THE PEOPLE ON PRIVILEGE HILL

THE PEOPLE ON PRIVILEGE HILL

AND OTHER STORIES

JANE GARDAM

Chatto & Windus
LONDON

Published by Chatto & Windus 2007

2 4 6 8 10 9 7 5 3 1

Copyright © Jane Gardam 1996, 2000, 2002, 2003, 2007

Copyright this edition © Jane Gardam 2007

Jane Gardam has asserted her right under the Copyright, Designs
and Patents Act 1988 to be identified as the author of this work

This edition published in Great Britain in 2007 by
Chatto & Windus
Random House, 20 Vauxhall Bridge Road,
London SW1V 2SA

www.rbooks.co.uk

Addresses for companies within The Random House Group Limited can be found at:
www.randomhouse.co.uk/offices.htm

The Random House Group Limited Reg. No. 954009

A CIP catalogue record for this book
is available from the British Library

ISBN 9780701177997

The Random House Group Limited makes every effort to ensure that the papers
used in its books are made from trees that have been legally sourced from
well-managed and credibly certified forests. Our paper procurement policy can be
found at: www.randomhouse.co.uk/paper.htm

Printed and bound in Great Britain by
Mackays of Chatham PLC

Contents

FOR KITTY

The People on Privilege Hill

Drenching, soaking, relentless rain. Black cold rain for black cold winter Dorsetshire. Edward Feathers loved rain but warm rain, falling through oriental air, steam rising from sweating earth, dripping, glistening drops that rolled across banana leaves, rain that wetted the pelts of monkeys. Bloody Dorset, his retirement home. He was cold and old. He was cold and old and going out to lunch with a woman called Dulcie he'd never much liked. His wife Betty had been dead some years.

'I am rich,' announced Feathers – Sir Edward Feathers QC – to his affluent surroundings. On the walls of the vestibule of his house hung watercolours of Bengal and Malaya painted a hundred years ago by English memsahibs under parasols, sitting at their easels out of doors in long petticoats and cotton skirts with tulle and ribbons and painting aprons made of something called 'crash'.

Very good, too, those paintings, he thought. Worth a lot of money now.

Under his button-booted feet was a rug from Tashkent. Nearby stood a throne of rose-coloured silk, very tattered. Betty had fallen in love with it once, in Dacca. Nearby was a brass and ironwood umbrella stand with many spikes sticking out of it. Feathers turned to the umbrella stand, chose an umbrella, shook it loose: a fine black silk with a

3

malacca handle and initialled gold band. He did not open it in the house on account of the bad luck this would unleash. A fresh wave of rain lashed at the windows. 'I could order a cab,' he said aloud. He had been a famous barrister and the sound of his voice had been part of his fortune. The old 'Oxford accent', now very rare, comforted him sometimes. 'I am rich. It's only a few minutes away. The fare is not the issue. It is a matter of legs. If I lose the use of my legs,' he said, for he was far into his eighties, 'I'm finished. I shall walk.'

Rain beat against the fanlight above the front door. There was a long ring on the bell and a battering at the knocker. His neighbour stood there in a dreadful anorak and without an umbrella.

'Oh yes, Veneering,' said Feathers, unenthusiastic. 'You'd better come in. But I'm just going out.'

'May I share your car?' asked Veneering. 'To Dulcie's?'

'I'm not taking the car.' (Veneering was the meanest man ever to make a fortune at the Bar except for old what's-his-name, Fiscal-Smith, in the north.) 'By the time I've got it out of the garage and turned it round I could be there. I didn't know you were going to Dulcie's.'

'Oh yes. Big do,' said Veneering. 'Party for some cousin. We'll walk together, then. Are you ready?'

Feathers was wearing a magnificent twenty-year-old double-breasted three-piece suit. All his working life he had been called Filth not only because of the old joke (Failed In London Try Hong Kong) but because nobody had ever seen him other than immaculate: scrubbed, polished, barbered, manicured, brushed, combed, perfect. At any moment of his life Feathers could have been presented to the Queen.

'Are *you* ready?' he asked.

'I'll take the anorak off', said Veneering, his scruffy old rival who now lived next door, 'when we get there. Don't *you* need a coat?'

'I have my umbrella,' said Feathers.

'Oh yes, I could borrow one of your umbrellas. Thanks.' And Veneering stepped in from the downpour bringing some of it with him. He squelched over to the Benares pillar and started poking about, coming up with a delicate pink parasol with a black tassel.

Both men regarded it.

'No,' said Feathers. 'That's a lady's parasol. Betty's.'

Veneering ran his arthritic fingers down the silk. Outside the rain had hushed. 'Just for down the road,' he said. 'I'd enjoy carrying it. I remember it.'

'It's not on offer,' said Feathers. 'Sorry.'

But Veneering, like some evil gnome, was over the doorstep again, introducing the parasol to the outer air. It flew up at once, giving a glow to his face as he looked up into its lacquered struts. He twirled it about. 'Aha,' he said.

Down came the rain again and Feathers, with a leonine roar of disgust, turned back to the umbrella-stand. Somewhere in the bottom of it were stubby common umbrellas that snapped open when you pressed a button. Right for Veneering.

'We'll be late,' said Veneering from the drive, considering Feathers's old man's backside bent over the umbrella-stand, floppy down the backs of his thighs. (Losing his flanks. Bad sign. Senile.) Veneering still had the bright blue eyes of a young man. Cunning eyes. And strong flanks. 'In fact we're late already. It's after one.' He knew that to be late was for Feathers a mortal sin.

So Feathers abandoned the search, checked his pockets for house keys, slammed the front door behind him and sprang off down the drive on his emu legs under an impeccable black dome, overtaking Veneering's short but sturdy legs, that thirty years ago had bestridden the colony of Hong Kong and the international legal world – and quite a few of its women.

Veneering trotted, under the apricot satin, way behind.

One behind the other they advanced up the village hill beneath overhanging trees, turned to the right by the church, splashed on. It was rather further to walk than Feathers had remembered. On they went in silence except for the now only murmuring rain, towards Privilege Road.

Dulcie's address was Privilege House, seat at one time, she said, of the famous house of the Privé-Lièges who had arrived with the Conqueror. Those who had lived in the village all their lives – few enough now – were doubtful about the Privé-Lièges and thought that as children they had been told of some village privies once constructed up there. Dulcie's husband, now dead, had said, 'Well, as long as nobody tells Dulcie. Unless of course the privies were Roman.' He had been a lawyer too and had retired early to the south-west to read Thomas Hardy. He'd had private means, and needed them with Dulcie.

There had been some Hardy-esque dwellings around

Privilege House with thatch and rats, but now these were glorified as second homes with gloss paint and lined curtains and polished door knockers. The owners came thundering down now and then on Friday nights in cars like Iraqi tanks stuffed with food from suburban farmers' markets. They thundered back to London on the Monday morning. Gravel and laurel had appeared around the cottages and in front of Dulcie's Norman demesne. A metal post said 'Privilege Road'. The post had distressed her. But she was an unbeatable woman.

Feathers paused at the top of the hill outside a cot (four bed, two bath) and called over his shoulder, 'Who the hell is this?' For a squat sort of fellow was approaching from a lateral direction, on their port bow. He presented himself into the rain as a pair of feet and an umbrella spread over the body at waist level. Head down, most of him was invisible. The umbrella had spikes sticking out here and there, and the cloth was tattered and rusty. A weapon that had known campaigns.

When it came up close, the feet stopped and the umbrella was raised to reveal a face as hard as wood.

'Good God!' said Veneering. 'It's Fiscal-Smith,' and the rain began to bucket down again upon the three of them.

'Oh, good morning,' said Fiscal-Smith. 'Haven't seen you, Feathers, since just after Betty died. Haven't seen you, Veneering, since that embarrassing little matter in the New Territories. Nice little case. Nice little milch cow for me. Pity the way they went after you in the Law Reports. Are you going to Dulcie's?'

'I suppose you're the cousin,' said Veneering.

'What cousin? I was a friend of poor old Bill till he dropped me for Thomas Hardy. Come on, let's keep going. I'm getting wet.'

In single file the three old judges pressed ahead: black silk, apricot toile and bundle of prongs.

Fiscal-Smith made uncouth noises that in another man might have indicated mirth, and they reached Dulcie's tall main gate, firmly closed. Through the wrought iron there was very much on view a lawn and terrace of simulated stone and along the side of the house a conservatory that was filled with coloured moons. They were umbrellas all open and all wet.

'Whoever can be coming?' said Feathers, who originally had thought he was the only guest. 'Must be dozens.'

'Yes, there *was* some point to the cousin,' said Veneering, 'but I can't remember what. She talks too fast.'

'It's a monk,' said Fiscal-Smith. 'Not a cousin but a monk. Though of course a monk *could* be a cousin. Look at John the Baptist.'

'A monk? At Dulcie's?'

'Yes. A Jesuit. He's off to the islands to prepare for his final vows. This is his last blow-out. She's taking him to the airport afterwards, as soon as we've left.'

Feathers winced at 'blow-out'. He was not a Catholic, or anything, really, except when reading the Book of Common Prayer or during the Sunday C of E service if it was 1666, but he didn't like to hear of a 'blow-out' before vows.

8

'*What* airport?' asked Veneering. 'Our airport? The airport at the end of the universe?' for he sometimes read modern books.

Feathers, who did not, suspected nastiness.

'Dulcie's a kind woman,' he said, suppressing the slight thrill of excitement at the thought of her puffy raspberry lips. 'Very kind. And the wine will be good. But she's obviously asked a horde,' he added with a breath of regret. 'There are dozens of umbrellas.'

In the conservatory trench six or so of them seemed to stir, rubbing shoulders like impounded cattle.

Feathers, the one who saw Dulcie most often, knew that the wrought-iron gate was never unlocked and was only a viewing station, so he led the way round the house and they were about to left-wheel into a gravel patch when a car — ample but not urban — pounced up behind them, swerved in front of them, swung round at the side door and blocked their path. Doors were flung open and a lean girl with a cigarette in her mouth jumped out. She ground the cigarette stub under her heel, like the serpent in Eden, and began to decant two disabled elderly women. They were supplied with umbrellas and directed, limping, to the door. One of them had a fruity cough. The three widowed judges might have been spectres.

'God!' said Fiscal-Smith. 'Who are they?'

'It's the heavenly twins,' said Feathers with one of his roaring cries. 'Sing in the church choir. Splendidly.' He found himself again defensive about the unloved territory of his

9

old age and surprised himself. When had Fiscal-Smith last been near a church? Or bloody Veneering? Never.

'Who's the third?' asked Fiscal-Smith. 'Is she local?'

'She'll be the carer,' said Feathers. 'Probably from Lithuania.'

'This is going to be a rave,' said Veneering, and Feathers felt displeased again and almost said, 'We're all going to get old *one* day,' but remembered that he'd soon be ninety.

A blaze of yellow light washed suddenly across the rainy sky, ripping the clouds and silhouetting the tree clumps on Privilege Hill. He thought: I should have brought something for Dulcie, some flowers. Betty would have brought flowers. Or jam or something. And was mortified to see some sort of offering emerging from Veneering's disgusting anorak and – great heaven! – something appearing in Fiscal-Smith's mean paw. Feathers belonged to an age when you didn't take presents or write thank-you letters for luncheon but he wasn't sure, all at once, that Dulcie did. He glared at Fiscal-Smith's rather old-looking package.

'It's a box of tea,' said Fiscal-Smith. 'Christmas-pudding flavour from Fortnum and Mason. I've had it for years. I'm not sure if you can get it now. Given it by a client before I took Silk. In the sixties.'

'I wonder what the monk will bring,' said Veneering. He seemed to be cheering up, having seen the carer's legs.

And here was Dulcie coming to welcome them, shrieking prettily in grey mohair and pearls; leading them to the pool of drying umbrellas. 'Just drop them down. In the conservatory trough. It's near the hot pipes. It's where I dry my dahlias. They love it. Don't they look pretty? Sometimes I think they'll all *rise* into the air.'

(She's insane, thought Feathers.)

'And I must run to my soufflé,' she called. 'Do go in. Get a drink. Awful rain. So good of you to come out. Introduce yourselves.'

In the sitting room there was no sign of the guest of honour. The carer was pouring herself an enormous drink. The cleaning lady of the village, Kate, was handing round titbits. She knew the guests intimately. 'I told you not to wear that shirt until I'd turned the collar,' she hissed at Veneering.

They all drank and the rain rattled down on the glass roof of the umbrella house. The clocks ticked.

'What's that over there?' asked Veneering.

A boy was regarding them from a doorway.

'A boy, I think,' said Feathers, a childless man.

'Maybe this is the cousin. Hello there! Who're you? Are you Dulcie's young cousin?'

The boy said nothing but padded after them as they carried their drinks into another room, where he continued to stare. 'Hand the nuts round,' said Kate the cleaner. 'Be polite,' but the boy took no notice. He approached Veneering and inspected him further.

'Why ever should I be Granny's cousin?'

Veneering, unused for many years to being cross-questioned, said, 'We understood we were to meet a cousin.'

'No. It's a monk. Do you play music?'

'Me?' said Veneering. 'Why?'

'I just wondered. I play cello and drums.'

'Oh. Good!'

'In America. I'm an American citizen. I don't come over often.'

'That explains everything.' (God, I'm hungry!)

'What do you mean?'

'Don't you say "sir" in America? I thought all American children were polite now.'

'Actually, not all. Sir. I know one who goes straight over to the fridge in people's houses and looks in to see what they've got.'

(Fiendishly hungry.)

'Would you have guessed I was American? I don't do the voice. I *can* do the voice but only at school. My parents are British. I won't salute the flag either.'

'You have a lot of confidence. How old are you?'

'I'm eight. But I'm not confident. I don't do anything wrong. I believe in God. I say my prayers.'

'I think we're all getting into deep water here,' said Fiscal-Smith, carrying away his gin-and-mixed. 'Off you go, boy. Help in the kitchen.'

The boy took no notice. He was concentrating on Veneering. 'Sir,' he said, 'do you, by any chance, play the drums?'

'*Off* you go now!' cried Dulcie, sweeping in and pushing the child under her grandmotherly arm out of the path of the three great men. 'This is Herman. My grandson. He's eight. I'm giving my daughter a break. Herman, pass the nuts.'

*

'My *wretched* monk,' Dulcie said. 'I don't think we'll wait. Oh, well, if you're sure you don't mind. The soufflé will be ready in about ten minutes and then we *can't* wait a *moment* more.' (Feathers's tummy rumbled.)

'But *do* you play the drums?' insisted Herman, circling Veneering before whose face hardened criminals had crumbled. Herman's face held up.

'I do, as a matter of fact,' Veneering said, turning away to take a canapé.

'They've given me some. Granny did. For my birthday. Come and see.'

And like Mary's lamb, Judge Veneering followed the child to a chaotic playroom where drums in all their glory were set up near a piano.

'I didn't know there was a piano here,' said Veneering to himself, but aloud. 'And a Bechstein.' He sat down and played a little.

Herman hove up alongside and said, 'You're good. I knew you'd be good.'

'Are you good?'

'No. Not at piano. I do a bit of cello. It's mostly the drums.'

Veneering, feet among toys, began to tap his toes and the Bechstein sang. Then it began to sing more noisily and Veneering closed his eyes, put his chin in the air and howled like a dog.

'Hey. Great!' said Herman, thumping him.

'Honky-tonk.' Veneering began to bob up and down.

'What's honky-tonk? D'you want to hear some drum-ming? Sir?'

'*Herman*,' called his grandmother.

'Better go,' said Veneering. Then he let his voice become a black man's voice and began singing the Blues.

'Better not,' said Herman. 'Well, not before lunch.'

The child sat close against Veneering at the table, gazing up at his yellow old face.

'Herman, pass the bread,' said Dulcie, but all Herman did was ask, 'Did you ever have a boy like me that played drums?'

'I did,' said Veneering, surprising people.

'After lunch can we have a go at them?'

'Eat your soufflé,' said Dulcie, and Herman obediently polished it off, wondering why something so deflated and leathery should be considered better than doughnuts or cake.

There was a pause after the plates were taken away and, unthinkably, Veneering, his eyes askew with gin and wine, excused himself and made again for the piano, Herman trotting behind.

'Oh no, I won't have this,' said Dulcie.

'America, I suppose,' said Feathers.

A torrent of honky-tonk flowed out of the playroom and some loud cries. The drums began.

Bass drums, floor-tom, normal-tom, cymbals. High-hat, crash-ride, thin *crash*! And now, *now*, the metallic stroking, the brush, the whispering ghost – listen, listen – and now the big bass drum. Hammers on the pedals, cross arms, cross legs, tap tap, paradiddle, paradiddle, *let go*! Hammer on pedal now then – HIGH HAT! CRASH RIDE! THIN CRASH!

The glass doors of the conservatory, now filming up, shook as if they'd received the tremors of a not-too-distant earthquake, and a new sound joined the drums as Veneering began to sing and almost outstrip the tremors. Not a word could be heard round the dining table and Dulcie rushed out of the room. As she left, came the crescendo and the music ceased, to reverberations and cackling laughter.

'*Herman!* Please return to the table. Don't dare to monopolise Judge Veneering.'

And Herman, staggering dazed from the mountain tops, let his small jaw drop and fell off his perch, scattering instruments.

Veneering sat on at the piano, hands on knees, chin on chest, enwrapped in pleasure. Then quietly, he began to play again.

'No – I'm sorry, Terry' – she had remembered his nasty little name – 'I'm sorry but I think the latecomer has just arrived. Come at once.'

There was a commotion going on in the hall.

'Dear Terry – *please*. It's boeuf bourguignon.'

Veneering jumped up and embraced her, grinning. 'Honky-tonk!' he said. 'He's good, that boy. Tremendous on the normal-tom. Could hear that bass a quarter-mile away. Beautiful brush on the snare.' He went back to the dining room rubbing his hands. 'Been playing the Blues,' he said to one and all.

'You haven't,' said Herman.

'Well, the Pale-Rose Pinks,' said Veneering. 'Near enough.'

'Veneering, more wine,' said Feathers warningly.

'Much better not,' said Fiscal-Smith.

The two damaged sisters sat, making patterns on the damask with their fingers.

'Hey! Could he play as well as me, your son?' asked Herman in an American accent.

There was a pause.

'Probably,' said Veneering.

'Did he make it? Was he a star? In music?'

'No. He died.'

'What did he die of?'

'Be quiet, boy!' Feathers roared.

'Now,' said Dulcie. 'Now, I do believe – here is our monk. Father Ambrose. On his way to St Umbrage's on the island of Skelt.'

'Bullet,' said Veneering. 'Soldier.'

'It's stupid to be a soldier if you can play music.'

'As you say. Quite so. Now, get on with your lunch, boy. We've plainsong ahead of us.'

But the plainsong was not to be. Nor did the monk join them for lunch. Kate the cleaner put her head round the dining-room door and asked to speak to Dulcie for a moment – outside.

And Dulcie returned with stony face and sat down, and Kate, unsmiling, carried in the stew. 'Take Father Ambrose's place away,' said Dulcie. 'Thank you, Kate. It will give us more room.'

Cautious silence emanated from the guests. There was

electricity in the air. In the very curtains. Time passed. The carer thought that she would kill for a cigarette.

'If he's not coming in, Granny,' asked Herman, loud and clear, 'can I have some more stew? It's great.'

Dulcie looked at him and loved him, and there was a chorus about the excellence of the stew, and Fiscal-Smith said it was not a stew but a veritable *daube* as in the famous lunch in *To the Lighthouse*.

'I've no idea,' said Dulcie grandly. 'I bought it for freezing. From the farmers' market, months ago. I don't think I've ever been to a lighthouse.'

'Virginia Woolf couldn't have given us a stew like this. Or a *daube*,' said one of the sisters (Olga), who had once been up at Oxford.

'She wasn't much of a cook,' said the other one (Fairy). 'But you don't expect it, when people have inner lives.'

'As we must suppose', Feathers put in quickly, before Dulcie realised what Fairy had said, 'this monk has. He is certainly without inner manners.'

Everyone waited for Dulcie to say something but she didn't. Then, 'Granny, why are you crying?' and Herman ran to her and stroked her arm. 'Hey, Granny, we don't care about the monk.'

'He – he suddenly felt – indisposed and – he vanished.' Her lunch party – her reputation as the hostess on Privilege Hill – gone. They would all laugh about it for ever.

Dulcie couldn't stop imagining. She could hear the very words. '*That* brought her down a peg. Asked this VIP bishop, or archbishop, or [in time] the Prince of Wales, and he took one step inside the house and went right out again. And she'd offered to drive him to the airport. What a snob! Of course, Kate knows more than she'll say. There must be something scandalous. Drunken singing and drums. African drumming. Yes – at Dulcie's. But Kate is very loyal. They'll all be leaving her a nice fat legacy.'

'A funny business. He probably caught sight of the other guests.'

'Or the dreadful grandson.'

Etc.

Then someone would be sure to say, 'D'you think there *was* a monk? Dulcie's getting . . . well, I'll say nothing.'

'Yes, there *was* someone. Standing looking in at them over that trough of umbrellas. Some of them saw him. Dripping wet.'

'Didn't he have an umbrella himself?'

'No. I don't think they carry them. He was wearing see-through plastic. It shone. Round his head was a halo.'

'On Privilege Hill?'

'Yes. It was like *Star Wars*.'

'Well, it makes a change.'

The story died away. The Iraq war and the condition of the Health Service and global warming took over. The weather continued rainy. The old twins continued to drowse. The carer had home thoughts from abroad and considered how English country life is more like Chekhov than *The Archers* or Thomas Hardy or even the Updike ethic with which it is sometimes compared. She would write a paper on the subject on her return to Poland.

But the startling image of the dripping monk remained with her. She felt like posting him an umbrella.

Kate, the ubiquitous cleaner, told her friend the gardener, 'Oh yes, he was real all right. And young. And sort of holy-looking.'

The gardener said, 'Watch it! You'll get like them. They're all bats around here.'

'I feel like giving him an umbrella,' Kate said. 'Wonderful smile.'

And one day Dulcie, in the kitchen alone with the gardener, Herman visiting Judge Veneering for a jam session, said, 'Don't tell anyone this, but that day, Father Ambrose in the rain, I kept thinking of Easter morning. The love that flowed from the tomb. Then the disappearance. I want to *give* him something.' She splashed gin into her tonic.

'Don't have another of those,' said the gardener to his employer.

Later, to old Feathers, who had called to present her with his dead wife's pink umbrella, having wrested it the day before with difficulty from Veneering, she said: 'I want to give him something.'

'Come, Dulcie. He behaved like a churl.'

'Oh, no. He must suddenly have been taken ill. I *did* know him, you know. We met at a day of silence in the cathedral.'

'Silence?'

'Yes. But our eyes met.'

'And he wangled a lunch and a lift?'

'Oh, didn't *wangle*. He wouldn't *wangle*. We talked for a few minutes.'

'A fast worker.'

'Well, so was Christ,' said Dulcie smugly.

Feathers, wishing he could tell all this rubbish to his dear dead wife, said, 'You're in love with the perisher, Dulcie.'

'Certainly not. And we're all perishers. I just need to fill the blank. To know why he melted away.'

'He probably caught sight of Herman.'

'How dare you!'

'No – I mean it. Monks have to keep their distance from small boys.'

And Dulcie yearned for her dear dead husband to kick Feathers out of the house.

'I have a notion to send that ... person in the garden – an umbrella,' said one twin to the other. 'I shall send it to Farm Street. In London. The Jesuit HQ. "To Father Ambrose, from a friend, kindly forward to St Umbrage on Skelt."' The other twin nodded.

Fiscal-Smith, who never wasted time, had already laid his plans. On his train home to the north on his second-class return ticket bought months ago (like the stew) to get the benefit of a cheaper fare, he thought he would do something memorable. Send the monk a light-hearted present. An umbrella would be amusing. He would send him his own. It was, after all, time for a new one. And he had had a delightful day.

Staunch fellow, he thought. Standing out there in the rain.

Veneering phoned Feathers to see if Feathers would go in with him on an umbrella for that fellow at Dulcie's on the way to the Scottish islands, the fellow who didn't turn up. Feathers said no and put the phone down. Feathers, a travelled man and good at general knowledge, had never heard of an island called Skelt or a saint called Umbrage. No flies on Judge Feathers. Hence Veneering because the pleasure of the lunch party would not leave him – the boy who liked him, the Bechstein, the drumming, the jam sessions to come – amazed himself by ordering an umbrella from Harrods and having it sent.

Five parcels were delivered soon afterwards to Farm Street Church. One parcel had wires and rags sticking out of it. And because it was a sensitive time just then in Irish politics, and because the parcels were all rather in the shape of rifles, the Farm Street divines called the police.

Old Filth was right. The Jesuits had never heard of Father Ambrose. So they kept the umbrellas (for a rainy day, ho-ho) except for Fiscal-Smith's. And that they chucked in the bin.

Pangbourne

I sit at my computer. It is my first. It is a present from the parish, and generous; for I am old and mad, and I do not look a natural for technology. I am not very friendly. My e-mail address is pangbourne.

This melancholy word has nothing to do with a place, or surname. It is the name of the great gorilla at our local zoo: the ape that has been the love of my life.

Pangbourne and I met soon after my marriage, when I moved down here to the blossoms and hops of Kent. I had married a Bounder, very late in life. He was after my money. There were terrible quarrels and, a creaking and distracted bride, I was soon to be seen trudging down Bekesbourne lane to Patrixbourne village, weeping.

Along the lane stands the zoo and one day at its gates appeared a huge banner: a four-times-life-size poster of a great gorilla. I was transfixed. It was love at first sight. I paid my five pounds and went in. And found him.

At once I knew that I must see him every day of my life and I arranged to donate almost every penny of my money to the zoo in return for free entry until my death.

The Bounder left me, shouting back at the house in the village street, 'You're unnatural, that's what you are. *You* are the gorilla. You've gorilla's hands.' That evening someone from the church brought me some flowers.

The Bounder was actually right. I have the hands of a gorilla. My fingers are thick as sausages and purple in cold weather. My nails are broad as postage stamps, my fingertips square, my knuckles an inch thick. I have read that the developing foetus passes through all the stages of God's creation. There is the insect, the reptile, the fish, the bird, the ape. You can see in many a human being the dominant stage of this development. The Bounder missed being a reptile by scarcely a hundred million years.

Something more extraordinary must have happened to my embryo, however, for though I am a small-boned little woman with a delicately shaped nose, and genteel and shapely feet, my hands seem to belong to somebody else. As a child I was not allowed piano lessons, I expect because they were embarrassed by my hands.

This day, the day of my great sadness, I have locked the door on myself and my computer (which inadvertently I manage deftly, swinging the mouse, flipping the paragraphs); I have locked myself in against watchers of my simian hands.

But it is strange that in all my eighty years nobody has ever said anything about my hands, except the Bounder.

The years have gone by. Every afternoon in all weathers, through sultry Augusts to black Kent Januaries when most of the animals kept to their lairs, I have walked the lane, carrying my little canvas stool. I have set it down outside the cage of Pangbourne.

The cage is vast. He shares it with his powerful extended family and also with some chimps who hurl themselves about above him, swing and drop at his feet or creep up from behind. Talking their heads off. He brushes them away with his iron hand and stares at something far beyond the zoo.

The crowds gather at the thirty-foot-high wire mesh and steel barrier, nose to nose with the notices that say 'These Animals Are Dangerous'. They say, 'Look! That's 'im. In 'e big? That's 'im on the poster. I wun like them fingers raan me neck.'

Pangbourne broods.

One of the things I've learned in the years we've been together: one does not look into a gorilla's eyes. I know his hot terrifying eyes only from an occasional sidelong glance. I have never caught him looking into mine.

Yet we are one.

It was many months before I addressed Pangbourne. It was on a bitter afternoon. Only the snow leopard and the wolves were out of doors. Not ape or monkey was to be seen, for even those born in captivity, like Pangbourne, hate the cold, and this was the coldest snap for years. I was so surprised and delighted to see Pangbourne wrapped loosely about with straw, in his usual place by the wire, the glorious inky core of him like a rock in a harvest field – his dear head that goes up to a point, his tongue and bald patch, his working jaw – that I cried out, 'Pangbourne! You are here!'

He was busy helping himself to sugar. A solution is kept filled up in a narrow pot hung inside upon the wire. All the apes take twigs and dip them in these pots, take out the twig and lick it. They are expert and dexterous, and the crowds love it. Pangbourne began to clean his yellow teeth with the twig, then nonchalantly threw it away. He yawned.

'I'm glad the sugar pot's not frozen,' I said.

He sighed, hugely, and looked away over my head at the jungles and shimmering mountains and the tropical flowers, the glitter of suggested snakes, the stirrings in the under-scrub and the silence above in the steaming forest canopy. His nostrils flared, searching for the sweet stench of rotting fern and the spice bushes. His eyes blinked at the metallic purple wings of butterflies the size of swallows that lived in his head.

'I've never seen any of that, either,' I said. 'I've not been out of England, myself.'

For a very odd moment Pangbourne looked at me and I knew he had the gist of it. He had no words, but he under-stood, and for months to come we conversed silently, paddling the two separate mulches of ideas that lurk word-less in the recesses of the brain, the mulch behind the word skills, drawn from the primeval soup. Once I wondered if Pangbourne was looking at my hands.

So the years passed.

I became almost an inmate of the zoo, sitting with my thermos of tea on my camp stool. As Pangbourne performed his party trick with the twig, he watched me at mine, unscrewing the top of the thermos and transforming it into a cup. The chimps provided the chorus, flinging themselves against the wire, trying to grab and tear, screaming like bad children. The gorillas sat about, unmoved. A blow from Pangbourne could easily kill. One snarling bite and the chimps would scatter, shrieking. And yet I knew him for a gentle beast and could have slept quietly in his arms.

Except when the public was near, I talked to my love all the time. The public did not often bother me, though they sometimes took photographs. I suppose I was rather a show for I had long ceased to care how I looked, except that, when not alone with Pangbourne, I always wore gloves.

One day Pangbourne wasn't there.

I waited an hour before I asked a keeper, who told me that the great ape had bronchitis. 'I must see him,' I said, and because I had given so much money to the zoo and expected one day to be commemorated on a plaque upon the gorillarium (like the poor keepers who over the years have been eaten by tigers and whose names are carved on a little cenotaph – with a space for more) he said that he would ask permission.

The next day – oh, what an agonised night! – he took me to Pangbourne's private chamber and there the great gorilla lay on a shelf with his face to the wall, his back (I now saw) silvery with age. He had a flannel blanket clutched round him like my old gran. I wanted to hug him and rock him and give him a peppermint. 'Pangbourne!'

'No. No closer,' said the keeper, but I knew that the gorilla had heard my voice.

*

He was out in the cage again by the spring, in the pale sunshine, but he had failed. He blinked a lot and swung his head – when he lifted it and tried to peruse the sky, soon he bowed down. He took no interest in the syrup supply.

I could not see for weeping.

Suddenly I thought to sing to him and, oblivious to the public and the chimps, I raised my voice in a hymn. 'We are travelling home to God,' I sang, 'in the way our fathers trod.'

I silenced the zoo! Pangbourne rolled forward in the straw and lay in a large loose heap. I never had a tuneful voice.

I drew on my gloves and went home.

I didn't attend the zoo after that for a full week. I had caught a nasty chest myself. I kept to my bed and missed church on Sunday. On the Monday morning someone called and said I was wanted up at the zoo and should she take me when I felt better. 'Please take me now,' I said.

'Yes,' they said at the zoo. 'Come this way please. The owner would like to speak to you,' and they took me to the owner's house up the curved white steps and under the spun-sugar portico.

He was the soul of kindness (well, I'd given him my every-thing) and said he wanted to tell me himself that Pangbourne was now very ill and must be 'put out of his misery'. He seemed sad. He took my hands – I had forgotten the gloves – and looked at them. 'What pretty hands.'

Together we walked to the gorillarium and Pangbourne still sat in the cage. 'I'll leave you together,' said the owner.

It was early in the morning, the public not yet admitted. The zoo lay still.

I had not my canvas stool with me and so I had to lean against the barrier fence as we are not meant to do. I took a very quick glance at Pangbourne, who was gazing as usual at the sky. A revelation came to me.

I bore him, I thought. All these years I have bored him. I have literally bored him to death.

But then the gorilla sighed and heaved himself together somewhat. Still without looking at me he felt around for a twig. After a pause he made a stab or two at the syrup bottle and fell back exhausted. Then he passed the twig to me through the bars.

Babette

When, some time ago, Babette's novel of before the war was reissued, the world went mad for it again. It flamed up in the bookshops and in the media, and sold in thousands to the reading groups. For a season it burned bright: book of the month, the week, the day, the moment. It was the book my mother and her friends had always doted on and which I had not therefore deigned to read. Now I read it and found it to be perfect. *Leafy Glades* it's called: a crazy, heartbroken, generous, funny, brave, piercing hymn to life. Babette had written other books, all forgotten. It was on the strength of *Leafy Glades* alone that she had earned the title 'Babette' – as it might have been 'Colette' or 'Fonteyn'.

But then she and *Leafy Glades* faded away. Their autumn had arrived. Winter fell.

Until now. So many years on came a new spring.

I reviewed the reprint of *Leafy Glades* for the *Times Literary Supplement*. Like every other reviewer, I assumed of course that Babette was dead. Long, long dead.

But there came a letter from the *TLS* and, inside it, another (pink) envelope with 'Kindly Forward' on it, and my name. Inside this was a scrap of toilet paper where a spider had been writing shorthand in violet ink. All I could make out was a phone number. Not even a signature.

I phoned up.

'Hi,' said a strong, hard voice. 'This is Babette. I am quite able to take your call at the moment if you will tell me, first, who you are so that I can decide if it will be worth my while. Please speak slowly after the tone. Oh, well, hello. I thought you'd ring. I'll be right over.'

'But you're –?'

'Dead? No. I'm living in Shepperton or Isleworth. Or somewhere. It's all one. I used to live somewhere near you, I think.'

'Oh yes. I know. I know the house. Not far from the church.'

'You didn't put that in your review.'

'Well, I tried to write about the book.'

'That's why I wrote to you. I want to give you a present. I shall come over and see you. And the old homestead.'

'I . . . can't I come and fetch you? And drive you home again?'

'*Drive* me? No. I've got my bus pass. I'm all of sixty now, you know, amazing as it may seem.'

'Yes. Well. But –'

'I'll be with you at twelve o'clock sharp.'

'Yes. Of course. When?'

'Today,' she said.

There she stood. My house has steep steps up to the front door and she stood below them on the gravel, bearing in her right hand a six-foot stave. I saw her begin to strike the ground with the butt of the stave, as if, at a given sign, it would pluck her up into the air and drop her on my doormat. I ran quickly down to her. She was a creature of tatters and wisps, in a long coat and none-too-clean balaclava helmet.

'Let's go,' she cried and set off towards the gate, me trotting behind, wishing for a muffler in the cool spring air.

There is all about the divine south London suburb in which I live a network of little passages thought to have once been the tracks around the edges of fields. They run now between fine gardens of many mansions. They are three feet wide and their clapboard walls are six feet high, flimsy and sometimes almost swaying in the wind. One can slink secretly about the town along these old sheep-runs. They are called 'The Slips'.

Dark things occur there and at night many a soul has wished that she had kept to the high street. Many a slip.

Babette stopped dead in the middle of the first Slip and examined the rich graffiti on the wooden walls. 'Do you remember that boy?' she said. 'He drew a crucifix here. He wrote beneath it "What a way to spend Easter". He's a bishop now.'

'No. I don't.'

'My son could get rid of all these,' she said of the graffiti. (Son? Babette? A family life?) 'He's a specialist with the airbrush, though of course he is retired now. Tell me – can one still hear –?' and she began to thump the stout oak on the tarmacadam among the condoms and the chickweed. 'Ah! *There!*' she said. 'You can still hear the little streams in the chalk that eventually reach the Thames.'

*

We came out among affluent mansions and palm trees bought at Harrods. Then we plumbed into the next Slip. Then another. Then we burst out near the church and opposite stood the tall sentry box of a house that I'd always heard had been Babette's.

'No blue plaque,' she said and I was surprised to see eyes full of tears. I could have died for her.

'It's too soon,' I told her. 'You're too young. You have to have been dead fifty years before you get a blue plaque.'

She gave me a look through the slit in the balaclava. 'Well, there it is,' she said. 'Place of my joys. He died, you know, my Romeo. He never left me. Two apartments under one roof. What is called a "successful conversion". Like St Paul. We were the top one. Only the roof above us. We got in at the side. Through a side door. The ground floor with the columns and the fanlight and the bust of Lord Nelson belonged to the Admiral and his wife. Dead of course, long ago. They looked like black beetles.'

At that moment the front door opened and two black beetles walked out hand in hand. When they caught sight of Babette, terrible fear came upon them and they hoofed it down the terrace and round the corner, registering unbelief.

'Still alive,' she said – Babette. 'Well, we gave them a good fright. Now, look. Before we moved we had to leave some treasures behind us. In the roof. We couldn't get them out through the side door. The Admiral and his dame could have obliged us. Through their front door. But they wouldn't hear of it. So we had to haul them up into the roof – it was before the fall of France – and we boarded up the opening. They'll still be up there. I'd like you to accept them.'

I asked what they were.

'Oh – a big Victorian rocking horse. An eighteenth-century doll's house. And a bathtub.'

'A doll's house tub?'

'A human's bathtub fit for Cleopatra. Indestructible. Cast-iron. White porcelain thick as your finger. Painted feet. Acanthus leaves. Worth a bomb now. Though what is a bomb worth? It's all yours if you want it.'

'You lifted a Victorian cast-iron bathtub into the roof?'

'We used block and tackle. My son was talented and strong.'

'But surely it will all belong to whoever lives there now?'

'I don't see why. I labelled them with my name and number and the new address, and "To Await Collection". It was scarcely fifty years ago. My telephone number is little changed.'

'But however could I get them out?'

'I'll write. But first we must make sure that they are still there. My son used to crawl up that drainpipe. When we lost our doorkeys. It still looks firm. See the little window under the eaves? Shin up and take a shufti.'

'You mean that you expect me to climb up the side of the house? Up . . . three floors? Up the drainpipe?'

'I don't see why not. You're young. Well, fairly young.'

'But I review for the *Times Literary Supplement*.'

We enjoyed this notion.

'I knew you were the one for my inheritance,' she said. 'I'm off now. Let me know how you get on.'

'But you were coming back for lunch.'

'All in good time,' she said.

But there was no good time.

There was no time at all.

A few weeks later a newspaper rang me to ask if I would write Babette's obituary.

'But she had years to go yet,' I said. 'I walked all the way round the town with her the other day.'

'Well, she's gone,' said the newspaper.

After a time I called at Babette's old house. I did not call on the Admiral and the Admiral's apartment because I had found lately that I was forever bumping into the pair of them taking the air on the Common and an expression I did not care for darkened the Admiral's beetle brow. I called instead at the side door.

Nobody answered, so I left a note asking the occupants of the top flat to call on me in Putney, and to my surprise they did. They were a serious but colourless couple and when I told them that there might be treasures in their roof they looked as embarrassed for me as if I had been reading too many children's books. They said they had heard that there had once been very mad people living in the house. A fat, middle-aged man used to climb up the drainpipes and the dear Admiral had watched muttering, 'Let him fall.'

'I believe there is a magnificent bathtub in your roof.'

They stared. 'Are you a friend of the family?'

'Oh *yes*,' I said.

They got up to go.

'There will be a blue plaque one day on your house,' I said. 'Babette was a genius. A wonderful novelist.'

'We don't read novels,' said the colourless couple. 'We believe in the quest for absolute truth.'

'That is where you might find it.'

'What — in a bathtub? In our roof?' And they scuttled away, having consumed a good deal of cake.

I decided that I had to climb Babette's drainpipe.

First I looked out my old catsuit.

Then I decided that I would perhaps attend a gym.

Then that I would choose the next but one most moonless night and to hell with the *Times Literary Supplement*. I would carry a torch between my teeth and under the eaves high above the treetops I would penetrate Babette's attic with light.

I never did.

For on the next moonless night — just as well I hadn't chosen it — the suburb resounded to the fall of Babette's house of joy.

Some great weight had fallen through the attic floor.

The weight had fallen first through the ceiling of the colourless couple, then through their floor, and the ceiling of the Admiral and his missus, bringing with it mouldings, staircases, chimney and the roof; and leaving four bodies one-dimensional in the dust.

There was no sign of the antique doll's house or the rocking horse that were rumoured to have been recently discovered and transported to a top dealer. It was said that there had been builders about, opening up ceilings. The four, now dead, occupants had been planning a cruise together. A bath, stubborn, immovable in the dark, they had had to leave. But it was now restless and had taken matters into its own hands and descended.

In the heap the bath raised its blunt head and was plucked out of the rubble like an oyster from chowder, and I am lying in it now.

The brass taps, the chain, the plughole, the plug now gleam with polish. I have painted the body of the bath blue and its acanthus feet turquoise, and it stands in the middle of my bathroom like a barque upon a lake, as in all the classy magazines.

I believe that Babette's bathtub, like Babette's one great novel, will last for ever and I lie in the steam and bubbles considering her, and all of us who try to write the truth.

The Latter Days of Mr Jones

I

The last of his tribe, the last of his kind, Mr Jones walked each day from his house next to the church up to the Common, as he had done for perhaps fifty years. He was well over eighty, upright, amiable, a military-looking man with the old soldier's legacy of highly polished shoes. He walked, had always walked, with a couple of dogs held taut on a single lead: Yeoman and Farmer. They had tails that curled briskly over their backs and optimistic eyes. It was said that if Mr Jones had had a tail and the dogs well-polished shoes, they would have made triplets. Alas. The last of the Yeomen and Farmers – generations of dogs had always had the same names – were gone. They had become too much for Mr Jones and had begun to pull him over now and then. He had had a fall by the pond. When the time came for the last couple to go Mr Jones did not replace them and he now strode forth with glazed eyes, brandishing only a walking stick. Some of his less sensitive neighbours stopped him to ask, 'No dogs, Mr Jones?' and he would stare them out and say, 'No, I'm afraid not,' and talk about the weather, which was one of his few topics.

When he reached the pond on the Common, Mr Jones always sat down on a long green seat. In one of the houses that stood on the edge of the Common there had been an infant school ever since he was a boy, and twice a day, even now, at break times its big door opened to disgorge children who all made for the pond with a particular kind of shrill and shouting music. This they kept up steadily for half an hour. 'Mr Jones, Mr Jones – how's Yeoman? How's Farmer?' They danced facetiously in front of him and crept up from behind the seat to pretend to throttle him. They quarrelled about who should climb on his knee and stroke his white moustache. When they became really tiresome a teacher came blowing her whistle in short, sharp blasts to say, 'That'll do. Stop it. Don't be unkind to Mr Jones.'

But he was the mildest of men and seemed unaware of anything the children did to him. He said little and drew back beneath his beetle brows, and stared across the Common at things the children had never seen and would never see.

Mr Jones was odd.

He lived in the house where he had been born, and his mother before him, in a road of Victorian mansions in a beautiful London suburb on a hill. He had been the youngest of a big family, all now dead. He had been 'educated at home' though the other Joneses had gone away to school. There were faded Victorian photographs in family albums of all the children gathered round Mr Jones in his pram, two uniformed nursemaids in attendance. Bonneted Mr Jones had watched the others flinging sticks into the pond, pushing each other over, falling in, yelling, bursting into tears, spitting and being smacked, then everyone laughing again. The winter when Mr Jones had taken his first tottery steps, bending with mittened hands to try to pick up snow, he still remembered. The setting sun balanced orange on the edge

46

of the Common sending immense shadows through the trunks of the pines had seemed to hesitate, trying to hold on to the last of the winter day.

Orange, black and white, Mr Jones remembered. Orange sun, the glossy blanket of snow and in the hollows at his feet in their little buttoned boots, black needles of grass pricking up through crisp rime. They were only glimpses now, but very vivid and the light of his life.

Now, children wore jeans and hunkish white sand-shoes at all seasons, or they were in tracksuits and he could not tell if they were boys or girls. They were all very fat and always eating. Nobody was shy and they made fun of the elderly. Sometimes when they came crawling round him and the dogs, he felt like reprimanding them, but he'd never had the knack of command. He had been less than three months in the army – though this was not generally known – because he could not obey orders at any speed and his commanding officer had sent for him one day to say that they felt that he would be happier as a civilian. A courteous man. He had known Mr Jones's father. So Mr Jones did only fire-watching duties through the Second War and helped his mother in the way that sisters had once been expected to do. Mr Jones's sisters had long left home to be New Women. They had cut off their hair. The eldest one had been a suffragette before he was born.

Mr Jones's mother had adored her youngest child from the start. 'My Baby Jones,' she said each time they brought him home from the Common. She lifted him from the pram and kissed him. 'You aren't quite like other people but you're a beloved son all the same.' In the schoolroom, until he was a young man, she had read to him from the shelves of children's books that had been in the family for generations. There was a first edition of *Alice*.

The whole house was much the same now as then. His grandparents would have recognised it, as they almost would have recognised the whole road, although the road had had its ups and downs.

There were, for example, no households now with five or six indoor servants, no tradesmen coming to take grocery orders twice a week. In 1940 the houses in the road had passed into the pallor of wartime and in 1941 two of them had been bombed to rubble. Then squatters had arrived. Then squatters were flung out. High rooms were partitioned with plywood into tenements. Then in the seventies one by one the houses began to be bought up and restored. Then more than restored, with every feature replaced at great expense. Cellars became underground garages with overhead doors that opened magically before their owners' cars had reached the bottom of the hill. Gardens became paved with pastel stone set round a single palm tree. Serpentine box bushes flanked each front door. The two bombed, rebuilt houses were now indistinguishable from the others.

The people in the houses were very different too. There were no servants living in, except for nannies who had apartments on top floors and cars to take the children to school. Husbands were not much in evidence except when out jogging early and late – in their ski-suits. They were called 'partners'. The women Mr Jones thought looked rather like rats. Anxious rats with frightening jobs in the City – or in several cities – and in what seemed to Mr Jones their late middle age they appeared in couture maternity clothes that emphasised their condition so grossly that he had to look away. Huge, set-piece firework parties took place at Guy Fawkes and Christmas and at Hallowe'en and Thanksgiving, for the road was now international, and the façades were covered in webs of fairy lights. His neighbours told him they could get him more than two million for his house, but he didn't seem to understand.

He managed very well, still under the discipline of his long-dead mother. A firm cleaned for him and did the garden, and another firm his laundry. The Jones money seemed to be holding out, managed (at a price) by a London solicitor. The church next door – 'My church,' he called it – helped with shopping, ran in with cakes and marmalade, looked after him when he was ill – which was almost never – and saw to his flu jabs. When he had been a sidesman for over fifty years the church bought him a television and video recorder, which he ignored. A neighbour asked what would become of the house when he . . . when he could no longer look after himself and Mr Jones said that it was left to the church, who planned to expand. He wanted to do something for the homeless.

The neighbours became less certain of the charm of Mr Jones after they learned about the homeless, and less certain still when their children joined the infant school on the Common and they discovered that Mr Jones sat watching them every afternoon.

II

One morning Mr Jones stood at his bathroom window, drying himself on a hard towel, and saw a policeman standing in his back garden.

Very odd.

He dressed and walked downstairs to the kitchen where he set the kettle on the stove, and the policeman was looking at him through the half-glazed kitchen door.

'Hello?' said Mr Jones, opening it.

'Good morning, sir. I came round the back. Didn't want to draw attention. Left the car on the corner by the church.'

'Come in. Would you like some tea?'

'No tea, thank you, sir.' The policeman looked into the distance, rather ill at ease.

'Is something the matter?'

'There have been complaints, sir.'

'About me? My accountant says we can have the house repainted next year.'

'No, sir.'

'I agree. It's a disgrace. I can't think what my mother –'

'It's about the children on the Common, sir. It's said you go there every day?'

'Yes. Yes, I do. For many years I am proud to say, in all weathers.'

'Just to look at the children, sir?'

'Oh yes. I have always been with children on the Common. I was the little one, you see. The youngest. A large family. All the rest of us are dead now.'

'You are very fond of children, sir?'

Mr Jones poured his tea and thought about it. 'As a matter of fact, no. Not of children per se.'

'Pure what, sir?'

'I'm not fond of people just because they begin as children. To tell you the truth I'm more fond of dogs. I miss my dogs. The children miss my dogs. I had to have them put down, you know.'

'I'm sorry, sir. But, if you don't care for children, why do you have to go and watch them every day?'

Mr Jones brooded and said he didn't know. 'They seem to like me. Since I was a baby,' he said, 'children won't leave me alone. I don't know why. Mother said that there are just some people like that. My brothers and sisters used to hug me all the time. Children follow me. Mother said that the famous novelist, Jane Austen – you may have heard of her – had the same trouble.'

'No, sir. I hadn't heard.'

'I don't like to tell them on the Common that I'm not really interested in *them*. I – you see, I tend to look at *ghosts*.'

'Ghosts, sir?'

'All the ghosts. The old ghosts. All gone now.'

'I have to ask you something, sir. Do you ever wish you could see the children in the nude?'

'In the *nude*? Of course not! I never ever saw my brothers – good gracious! I never saw my sisters – my *mother* – oh, good gracious!'

'I'm afraid I have to warn you, sir. It's the climate of the times.'

'I don't take *The Times*, I take the *Daily Telegraph*.'

'Have you a solicitor, sir? Just in case.'

The following Sunday Mr Jones hung about after the church service until the coffee was finished and the coffee ladies had washed all up. The vicar, seeing him, was worried. 'Care to come back for a bite of lunch, Mr Jones?' and his wife said, 'Oh yes, please do. It's only fish pie, but come.'

'Delighted,' said Mr Jones, but spoke hardly a word. He did not seem hungry.

Afterwards she said, 'Mr Jones – what's wrong? Go and talk to George while I clear up.'

'Trouble?' asked the vicar.

'A policeman came,' said Mr Jones.

'I'd heard something,' said the vicar.

'Said I mustn't watch the children on the Common. I can't think why. I always did. Some people watch the tennis. Now people seem to be keeping away from me.'

'I'll fix it,' said the priest, and went down the hill to the station on the Monday morning.

'I'm not having this,' he told them. 'Right? I've known Jones for years. We all know him. He's an innocent.'

'It's with the Crown Prosecution Service now, sir. It's out of our hands. There've been allegations.'

'Of what?'

'Come in here, sir, for a minute. There have been allegations of gross indecency. About forty years ago. A woman of fifty has alleged rape. When she was eight. On the Common. Persistent rape. A hundred times in three months.'

'*Mr Jones?*'

'You'd be surprised, sir.'

'Nothing surprises me. Was this woman in therapy? Going through the menopause? Useless husband?'

'Something of the sort, sir,' said the policeman, surprised.

'They so often are,' said the vicar. 'Wanting to find a reason for an unsuccessful life. "Nothing ever came up to my lovely childhood" – destroyed by a pervert. Tripe. We're only just beginning to learn about the memory. And the powers of suggestion. Innocence is not considered.'

'I'm afraid there are quite a lot of allegations, sir. One woman seems to have jogged the memories of others. We've been working on this case for a long time. The neighbours are not happy. Some of them have children.'

'The Common is where Mr Jones feels safe. You must see he's a bit strange. A lonely man. One on his own.'

'It'll be his only hope, sir. "Diminished responsibility." Otherwise it's going to be – well, you know – a custodial sentence.'

'Send Mr Jones to prison? At eighty-three!'

'Look in the papers, sir.'

'The police have gone mad.'

The inspector walked the vicar to his car and said, 'Look. Now we're alone. Listen. I wonder if you realise the filth the police have to face? The videos? The Internet muck? You don't hear of what it does to the police. You don't hear of the nervous breakdowns. Do you think the police *enjoy* it? The foul age we live in?'

'All ages are foul. All ages are also glorious. And Mr Jones has no videos and no Internet. No child has been across his doorstep.' And he drove away.

'Priests have to watch it,' said the inspector, 'as we know full well.'

Half an hour later Mr Jones opened the door to the vicar, shaky, but immensely pleased to see him. They sat in the schoolroom, the priest with his back to the shelves of children's books. 'Mr Jones,' said the priest, 'I'll stop this if it's the last thing I do. I can't have policemen calling here and going for you.'

'He was a decent man,' said Mr Jones. 'I didn't know what he was saying.'

'Before I take this to hell and back,' said the vicar, 'tell me this. We don't go in for the Sacrament of Confession at our church, do we? We are Low. You know that?'

'Oh yes. My mother was always Low.'

'I want you, even so, to treat this talk we're having as secret as the Confessional. Answer me, Jones, as you will have to answer on the Dreadful Day of Judgement. Tell me the absolute truth. Have you something to tell me that frightens you? Of which you are ashamed? That troubles you deep down in yourself? That you do not understand?'

Mr Jones stared his blue stare for a long time. He seemed to be trying to read the titles of the books behind the vicar's head. 'Yes,' he said at last. 'I have.'

There was silence.

'I am troubled. I have always been troubled somewhere.

I think it is a sort of shame. Yet I don't know why. I could never talk about it. My father died when I was eight. I could never have asked Mother.'

'Go on.'

'Well. I can't understand what is meant by "sexual urges".'

'Sexual urges of any kind?'

'Yes. You see, they don't happen to me. And I'm afraid that what I understand of them disgusts me. It was the only thing about the dogs I did not care for. On the Common. Yeoman. Oh, I could not even think about it!'

'And your childhood?'

'Oh yes. I understand childhood. I've always wanted childhood again. I'm so sorry.'

The priest stood up, put his hand on Mr Jones's shoulder and said, 'God bless you. We'll blast them all to hell.'

It was Christmas time and at eight o'clock one morning there was a ring at Mr Jones's doorbell, and eight policemen were on the steps and police cars prominent in the road. A handcuff was fastened on to Mr Jones's wrist and its other link round one of the policemen's. Two policemen went upstairs and two more disappeared into the schoolroom. 'We have to ask you to come to the station, sir.'

Mr Jones had just finished breakfast and had not yet put on his shoes. He turned pale as his moustache. 'I am still in my slippers.'

'Slippers will do, sir. Do you want to sit down for a moment?'

'I have to ... I have to go to the WC.'

'You can go at the station, sir.'

'It is urgent. I have just had breakfast and I am well brought up. I am like clockwork. There will be an accident.'

They removed the handcuff and the lavatory door key and let him go in. 'Don't pull the chain, sir.'

Then they took him away to charge him, offering to contact his solicitor. Mr Jones could not remember the solicitor's name. It would not come. 'I must see my parish priest. He will want to be here.'

'We'll let you see him later. First you must hear the charges made against you. Shall we read them out to you?'

'I am able to read.'

But reading, he did not understand.

'Do you want to sign these allegations, sir?'

'I want to see my parish priest.'

Four hours later, he was given a cup of tea. Mr Jones was allowed home. The handcuff was not restored. 'We'll drop you on your doorstep, sir. The padre will be there looking out for you. We found him. You're staying with him tonight.'

Mr Jones stared.

'We've insisted, sir. It's usual. We don't want you doing something foolish. By the way, don't forget that we'll need your passport. Get the padre to bring it in.'

'I have no passport. I've never been abroad.'

'Here we are then, sir. There's the light on – he's there.'

The wonderful familiarity of the front door. The brass bell and letter box. The door was on the latch.

But inside the house felt different. Antiseptic. The kitchen dresser, the wardrobe in the bedroom, the bathroom cupboards, some slightly open, had a self-consciousness he had not seen before. The downstairs lavatory door stood open and a rubber glove lay on the floor.

'Mr Jones? Hello? Is that you? Don't come in here –'

But it was too late. Mr Jones went into the schoolroom and saw that all the children's books were gone, and only then did he burst into tears.

III

After the police search of Mr Jones's house, and the charges made that he had been once a rapist, they left him to himself for some months, only requiring that he did not leave his premises overnight without informing them of his whereabouts. Mr Jones never went anywhere overnight and was only persuaded once or twice to stay at the vicarage or with a parishioner when faceless grey men with cameras began to hang about his gate. This happened on the occasions when he had to appear at a more important police station and then at the Crown Court. His solicitor was changed to one more used to crime and he found a Silk who specialised in this sort of case. This was a woman so busy that she hardly saw Mr Jones but said they would meet properly at the trial. Mr Jones looked at her with mild interest. She reminded him of one of the more forceful of the whistle-blowing teachers at the infant school who had apparently told the police, 'We never quite took to him.'

'The QC is very good,' said the vicar. 'So we hear.'

Mr Jones thought that she hadn't looked particularly 'good', but certainly strong and determined. Obviously he was not the easiest client because he was finding speaking more and more difficult. At one point the magistrates asked if he was deaf. It was the vicar who stood near him in the dock and answered the questions, Mr Jones observing the scene in silent and bewildered dignity.

The legal steps went forward steadily for several more months before the trial. The press came and went at the gate. At each court appearance there was now a report in the Surrey newspapers and a footnote or two in the *Guardian* where he was described as a pensioner, grey-haired and tall. The year drew to its end.

Mr Jones still walked on the Common but now went round two sides of a triangle to avoid the pond and the long seat. He walked out beyond the pine trees and the site of the old Roman fort where he could hear the steady throb of the motorway along Ermine Street. As a sort of comfort and passport he carried the dogs' lead. He avoided people with children. Sometimes a child who had known him ran up to him and he would turn his back and shout into the distance, 'Yeoman? Farmer? Here, boys, here.' People with dogs smiled at him and on the far tracks through the woods riders on horseback sometimes reined up and spoke to him. 'Take care out here on your own, sir. It's getting late. You can easily get lost. There are nasty people about.'

'I know every inch of the Common,' said Mr Jones. 'I'm never afraid.'

But most days he was invisible; lurking inside his house. Sometimes he even missed Sunday church, which was why it was not until Christmas time that he caught on to the news that his vicar was moving to a parish in the north of England. Mr Jones said nothing, but after Evensong that dark night he was seen by the vicar's wife standing across the road from the vicarage in the rain. She ran out without her coat, pulled him into the house and in the little hallway held his cold, gloveless hands. The vicar appeared and said, 'Oh God! We've prayed, we're still praying that this ridiculous business will be dropped before we leave. We didn't want you to know we were going until you're settled again. Mr Jones, we shall not *ever* desert you. I shall be at your trial. I promise.'

'Trial?'

He told Mr Jones (yet again) the date fixed at Quarter Sessions. He reminded him there would be a jury. He said that his Counsel was excellent. That there was money enough to pay her. That everyone was totally supporting him.

'I'm not sure,' said Mr Jones.

'Stay with us tonight.'

But Mr Jones preferred to go home.

In the rain, now turned to sleet, he went padding away and as he came to the church he saw that there were lights inside it. The Christmas lights, for it was still Epiphany, the feast of the Three Wise Men at Bethlehem. Turning off church lights had been his dominion for half a century and his reaction was immediate and automatic. This was somebody else's disgraceful negligence. He turned into his house where there was still a church key behind the front door next to the dogs' lead and hurried back again. He unlocked the church, switched on the light inside so that he would be able to see his way out again, as he had done a thousand times. He walked down the south aisle to switch off the tree. How very careless. How dangerous. Never happened before. And the light inside the Christmas crib was on, too, and the usual torch hidden in the hay around the holy family. The whole church could be ablaze by morning.

A barefoot child was looking at the crib. He was examining in his hand one of the little carved kings.

'How *dare* you!' Mr Jones astonished himself with a parade-ground voice. 'What are you doing here? This is holy ground. You behave as if you owned the place. Put down the Wise Man.'

The child replaced the figure in the stable, and disappeared.

The weather worsened. Mr Jones kept within doors. Some people began to be kind. They left him Christmas cake and mince pies and leftovers from the turkey at his back door. One or two of the grand neighbours even asked him to their New Year's parties. He did not reply. The vicar's farewell party in the church hall took place without him. The vicar sent letters from his new parish, and reminded him that he was not alone and would not be alone at his trial.

The neighbours began to notice an extended darkness over Mr Jones's house. The curtains stayed drawn in the daytime. There was scarcely a light. Nobody answered the doorbell. Someone among the grand neighbours said at a party that they had seen the police raid. Hundreds of pornographic books had been seized. Someone else said they had heard that Mr Jones believed he was Jane Austen, and one of the male 'partners' said that he had been jogging one evening just after Christmas and Mr Jones had burst out of the church shouting, 'I have seen the Christ, the Son of the Living God.' Or something of the sort.

'Mad,' they said. 'But if it's not true what they say about him . . . If the jury like him – he's a charmer after all – and he gets off, he's going to collect a fortune for slander.'

'It won't help him,' said another man of the world. 'There'll always be a question mark.'

Just before the feast of the Holy Innocents and a couple of days before Mr Jones's trial – and the day, incidentally, when all the charges against him were dropped because the main complainant remembered the attentions had really come from a long-dead uncle – Mr Jones went up to bed as usual.

The telephone had been ringing all day, but he had ignored it. He had polished his shoes and put them as usual at the foot of the stairs. He had drawn back his bedroom curtains and opened the window an inch as he always did. The night was black, heavy with coming snow. He climbed into his schoolboy bed and wished that his face would stop twitching and his heart thundering. He wondered where the vicar was. Obviously not coming. He wondered where his mother was. He wanted to tell her about the boy. It was like one of her stories. He wished the dogs were here. He slept.

There was a scratching at his bedroom door.

'Hello?'

Then a woof.

'Hello?' he shouted. 'Yeoman?'

He put on his dressing gown and slippers and opened the door. Nothing. Only the red and blue turkey stair-carpets and the brass stair-rods and the hall in darkness below.

'Hello? Farmer? Yeoman?'

From the other side of the front door a sharp bark. He rushed downstairs, kicked aside his shoes, opened the door upon the snowy front garden and in the road beyond he thought he saw them. He seized the lead, ran down the steps and into the road, which was lightly painted, white on black. There were no lights anywhere. It was about three o'clock in the morning. He ran up the hill towards the Common shouting 'Yeoman!'

At the top of the road he saw the pair of them watching him, then they turned to make for the pond. And there by the long seat they were waiting for him. He sat down jubilantly on the seat and died.

The early joggers found him at about seven o'clock in the morning shawled in snow, like a baby sleeping. 'Best thing that could have happened,' they said. They had not heard that there was to be no trial. They got on their mobiles and waited solemnly for the police and ambulance. The snow fell fast and lovely all around. They looked sometimes over their shoulders and the quiet Common beyond seemed peopled for miles by the joyful dead.

The Flight Path

J im Smith, not yet eighteen, had won an interview for a place at a London medical school, one of the great hospitals of the world. He was jubilant and at first unbelieving. The year was 1941. The London blitz was in full swing. Jim lived in the north-east of England and had not been south in his life. When the telegram came his mother flew into high hysterics, and ran up and down the street knocking on doors to inform the neighbours. Pale yellowish-orange, the telegram flapped in her hand.

How could he possibly go to London next week? There was no time to think out where he could stay, for London was too far for anyone to go and return on the same day. The furthest he'd been was Scarborough as a child, when they'd taken rooms for a summer holiday, the landlady cooking so long as they did the shopping and were in bed by ten. Two pounds ten the week.

And London now! The evening vigil round the wireless for the BBC News confirmed whispers and rumours, reading between the lines in the newspapers, and letters from the south: most nights London was end-to-end ablaze. The solemn voices of the newsreaders – Alvar Liddell, Bruce Belfridge – were echoed in the voices of the millions who talked together in fish queues across the nation.

It was midwinter. Blackouts were ritually fastened to every

window by four o'clock. Fires were small, for coal was short and the only heat-giving flames were the infernos of the great cities and, above all, of London, blasted by each fall of masonry as streets came tumbling down. In the Vale of York, Jim Smith's old father, wounded over twenty years earlier in the war before, wheezed in his chair, set his chin against his chest and ruminated. That morning he had read the *Daily Sketch* from cover to cover. It had not taken long for it was so thin. Some columns had been partly blacked out and others left white because of the mysterious Fifth Column always over one's shoulder. Smith had sat on, saying nothing. Jim, his only child, was clever and good, solidly northern and up to now untried by life.

'I'll write to Nell,' said Mrs Smith. 'After all, she's my first cousin once removed. She lives at London somewhere. I have the address for Christmas cards, not that there are any any more. Yes, Nell. She was always very nice. I expect she'll still be alive.'

But there arrived another telegram in reply to Mrs Smith's carefully written, perfectly spelled letter, neatly blotted and signed 'Your affectionate cousin Mrs Elizabeth Smith', crossed out and rewritten 'Betty'.

REGRET, said the telegram, IMPOSSIBLE STOP CISSIE VERY POORLY STOP NELLY.

'Who the hell is Cissie?' asked Mr Smith, lifting his gaze from the hearthrug and the parchment drum near the poker, which was decorated with hideous barbola work, lashed through punched holes with slanted leather laces and filled with paper spills to light cigarettes and save matches. 'Cissie who?'

'Well, it'll be Nell's father's sister's girl. His side some-where. I can't place her quite. She must be a hundred. Unless she's the other side altogether, married to the dentist, but he must be dead. Must be. Bobbie, he was, with a flickering eye. Yes, I suppose he could have married a Cissie. She had some-thing wrong with her reactions.'

'Bugger them both,' said Mr Smith. 'Bugger them all.'

But the next day came the third telegram of the week.

CISSIE BETTER STOP CONVENIENT FOR VISIT.

The Smiths considered the obvious dismay the request for a bed must have caused, the great discussion, the reluc-tant retraction. And Mrs Smith all at once recalled Cissie's mingy little face, lace handkerchief to nose and brimming stupid eyes. 'Nelly's had to work hard at them,' she said. 'Out of pure shame. To think they said no! We haven't seen them for years and I'm sure I don't want to, but to say *no*! You never say no to a relation! Well, I'll send them some ham. Under the counter from Ramshaw's farm. That'll shame them some more.'

Jim Smith in his world apart listened to all this with little interest. He had already made his arrangements for the night in London. His Maths teacher had given him an address near King's Cross Station, which was apparently very central, B&B, three shillings. The sheets would be pea-green flannelette, he was told, and he might not be the first to sleep in them since they last saw the wash tub and he'd probably have to share the room with several more, but there'd be two eggs for breakfast.

'Two eggs? Whoever can get two eggs? Not even my mother –'

'Some can,' said the Maths master. 'Those with connections. In King's Cross there's plenty of comings and goings.'

Jim Smith had thought that King's Cross was merely a railway station. He hadn't imagined that people lived in it. The Maths teacher had flat feet and spectacles heavy enough to absolve him from the armed forces. He was teaching PE, Religious Knowledge (Scripture) and Woodwork as well as Maths but still had time for meditation. 'Some give and some receive,' he said. 'You'll notice that soon. There are the getters and the givers. You can see it from birth – which child stretches out to share its rusk, which grabs. Never changes.'

'But', wailed Mrs Smith, 'you *can't*! I've arranged everything with Nelly now. Look at me when I'm speaking to you, Jim Smith, and not over my head. You're not a doctor yet. I still say what goes in this family and I'm doing my best. It's a safe address outside the East End of London and the bombs, along the railway line south-west. Nelly's a lodger in the house. The house is Cissie's and the dentist's. She never had any money, Nell. She's always been a tenant somewhere. Lived by her wits. She's a great organiser. She lost her fiancé in 1916 like many another. She hates rows. And she'd *never* have made illness an excuse. She's shamed them into having you. Shamed them. I always liked Nell. Oh, I feel better now.'

*

So the pea-green sheets and two eggs faded, never to be experienced, and Jim Smith monosyllabically set off, to find that King's Cross was more than a railway station and the station itself heavily disguised by sandbags bulging high and grey, like every other serious building around it. A taxi took him to the historic hospital, also sandbagged and so shabby it looked as if it was being closed down, its windows painted black, its corridors dirty and rubble in the drab grass outside. He found the interview room where five tired-looking men questioned him for a not very taxing half-hour. They said that his written papers and school results had struck them as outstanding. Was he about to be called up?

He said he was waiting to hear but had been told it was very unlikely and they all politely looked away from the thick glasses that had bonded him to the Maths teacher. The five tired men could see themselves, grey and old, reflected in Jim Smith's glasses in what in the London afternoon passed for light. They asked him if he had applied to other hospitals. Perhaps nearer home?

'No, sir.'

'Why is that?'

'I don't know. All up my way say Edinburgh's the place for Medicine but I've always fancied London.'

Silence. Thought.

'You are truthful,' said one of the five great men of the selection board. 'We are flattered.'

Jim wondered whether he was being mocked.

'You are, then, serious about coming here? Maybe quite

soon? Hospitals stay put, you know. They don't get evacuated like ministries and boarding schools.'

'Yes,' said Jim. 'As soon as possible. Well, naturally, very
proud indeed,' and his glasses flared.

Good.

The blitzkrieg on London was in its twenty-third night
and the great men all lacked sleep. Their hospital overflowed.
To find his interview Jim had had to sidle round rows of
patients lying in corridors, along landings and in what looked
like cupboards. He had come to the place through what must
be the City, whose black ruins smouldered. Fearful dark
cisterns the size of bungalows were filled with stinking
standing water covered by broken nets thick with ash.

Outside the hospital all this was now dark and the sirens
began to wail. Jim Smith winced.

'You haven't heard sirens?' one man asked.

'No. At home we get a phone message and my father or
Mr Parsley goes round the village on his motorbike blowing
a whistle.'

'Ah,' said the central figure behind the desk. 'Now you
are hearing our Angelus. It's time to go.'

They were gathering up their papers. They shook hands
with him. 'We look forward to seeing you next term.
Congratulations.'

'You mean I've got in? Can I tell people?'

They were hurrying into their coats. 'Yes, yes, indeed you
can.' They were making for the door. The more distant howls
of the sirens began to be joined by nearer ones, like wolves
across snow. Insolent and chilling, they ululated up and down.

'Off you go,' said the last of the great men in the doorway, fastening a briefcase. 'Getting home tonight I hope? Not too wise to stick about round here perhaps.'

'I'm going to . . . out to the suburbs. To family.'

'Excellent. We wouldn't want to lose you just as we've met. Off you go. Au revoir.'

In a moment he stood alone in the room. 'I'll be back,' he told it. 'You'll see.'

It took time to find his way out of the great grey place, at first down the crowded corridors lit only along the floor with blue lights, then across courtyards, into corridors lined with stretchers, running people, slamming swing doors muffled by hard asbestos sheets. He pushed on and into the inferno outdoors.

But outside there was no inferno. All was quiet as the country at home. The sirens had stopped and the white moon shone down on empty streets.

Where had everyone gone? The whole of London must be inside the hospital. The milky moonlit streets were white except for the arches behind the water tanks, which were black. Hardly a soul to see it. Hardly a soul except in the distance voices shouting about lights: 'Turn that bloody light off!', '. . . light off . . .', '. . . lights.' Shepherds across the meadows. The sky was scattered with stars.

He found an Underground station. The ticket office was empty. The escalators were not working and were blocked, and he set off down metal stairs that corkscrewed into the dark. As he clattered down deeper, down a second fire-escape stair, and a third, a sharpness about him turned into a smell that lapped him from far below, and grew stronger and sourer. He became aware of a distant starling chatter from some pit in the dark. Light began to filter up from below. It spread and the noise grew louder.

He stepped off the metal stair at last on to what must be an Underground platform; but none of it was to be seen for the confusion of bundles and bodies and blankets. Talk, talk. A shout or two. A crying child. Laughter. Away towards the blackness of the tunnel mouth someone was playing a squeeze-box. Jim Smith, after standing still a while, began to pick his way among the bundles and the shadows dotted with the red points of lighted cigarettes. Smoke from a thousand gaspers hit his throat. Black lips shining, red-black lips. Turbaned blonde heads with chunks of hair in boxy curlers, lumpy like Christmas stockings. Somebody knitting. A child desperately crying on and on. Tonight with all these unknown people might be the last of his life.

The stench of the blanketed bodies was sweetish, smelling of sweat and fry. Jim Smith clattered around kerosene stoves and pans, knocking over a squat whistling kettle. Somebody squawked at him but nobody swore. Jumping the hippo bundles, he began to be afraid and a scrawny arm stretched up from a bed roll, like a feeler. 'Lie here with me, boy.'

He shook her away, leaned his back into the concave white wall and a warm blast of wind puffed out of the tunnel mouth followed by a roar and he was pinned against the slippery tiles. The squeeze-box stopped. Several people stood up and a lighted train sprang out of the tunnel like a dragon arriving in hell.

When it stopped quite ordinary clean people stepped out, wide awake and carrying briefcases and gas masks on strings across their shoulders. All the men wore hats, the women gloves. There were no children. They stepped down among the permanent residents along the platform, like bathers into a shoal of fish, and nobody paid any attention until three airmen emerged, two with pilot's wings. A cheer went up, at first faint, then vigorous, and drifted in waves about the platform, louder then softer, louder then softer, like the sirens. The airmen gave the V for Victory sign and tried looking jaunty. One had bandaged hands and Jim Smith wondered if he was on the way to his hospital.

On the front of the train, miraculously, had been the word Wimbledon, and Wimbledon was Nell's address. Jim Smith stepped in.

Fore and aft he was pressed into a host of silent people pointedly looking away from each other and clinging to leather nooses that hung down from the roof. The people all rocked with the train. Within six inches from Jim Smith's face an old Jewish-looking man was observing him. He had never met a Jew, but he knew them from films. The horrors of the build-up to the war in Germany had almost passed Jim Smith by – he had been at school, minding his books – but he knew from somewhere that we must be nice to all Jews because of their rejection in this country over history when Jews could not ever own land. His father had said, 'How can we judge? In the Vale of York we have never met one. We have never owned land ourselves.' Jim Smith, looking so intimately now into the eastern face, asked politely of the old man if he knew how many stops there were before Wimbledon. The Jew told him (his breath was spicy). 'And', he said, 'I think you are from the north of England? Are you staying down here? Have you somewhere to go?'

'Only tonight. Then I'll get home. I'm staying with some relations.'

'Be glad of your relations, my boy. But one night here, with or without them, will suffice. You – in Wimbledon, down the hill, not up on the Common – you will be on the flight path.'

'I don't know whether it's up or down. I'll be OK,' said Jim Smith and the Jew held out his hand. Jim took it.

But there was no sense of impending danger when he stepped out of the train. Wimbledon Park seemed down the hill, almost in the fields. There were a few bundles in bed rolls on the platform and places were being reserved courteously for late arrivals. Quite respectably dressed and la-di-da (to Jim) different-sounding people were preparing food and the cigarettes were no longer Capstans and Woodbines but Players. There was less coughing but no squeeze-box. There was even the smell of some sort of coffee.

Jim Smith stepped out upon a boulevard of houses that stood tranquil under the same moon as in the broken city. He walked uncertainly past mansions unknown even to Scarborough. A dog or two ran by. Soon the streets began to run uphill to his right. One was sealed off with barbed wire and nearby some of the red tall houses were missing, a hole in the ground where cellars had been now filled with black water. A red and white sign said UNEXPLODED BOMB. It was neatly painted and you felt the enormity of such desecration in an ordered place. This was a street where you would not rush up and down showing people telegrams. Money, decorum, reticence were here; smugness probably.

He found himself standing at the end of Auntie Nell's road and walked a little way up the hill until he came to number 34 which was also labelled 'Hilly Mead', a huge tall house that loomed over him. A house he thought that must have had a servants' entrance. Until 1939 servants in uniforms would have been on their knees each morning washing down the wide front steps, polishing the big brass nipple of a bell, the heavy brass dollop of a door knocker. Not now. The porch's mosaic tiles needed clearing of litter and a good scrub. The letter box was tarnished and hung loose. Aunt Nellie must be different from his mother, who would have been out with a bucket and polishing cloth herself and hang what the neighbours thought, flight path or no flight path. Thinking of his mother, he wanted most desperately to be back at home.

But he rang the bell and after a time a faint light under the door went out. The door opened and in the shadows stood his mother.

She was smaller and had neater hair, and the hand she laid on his sleeve had polished nails and she smelled of scent, but the voice, the stance, were his mother's. 'Oh – hullo, Auntie Nelly? I'm Jim.'

'Well!' said the woman who at once was not his mother but her cousin Nell. 'So you're here! You'd better come in. It's a clear night, I'm afraid. The raid will start soon. You may not get your interview tomorrow if they hit the main line again. You'll be stuck here. Buses are hopeless. That's what we're all afraid of for you.'

'Mum sent me with my ration book in case. Oh yes, and some ham. I've had my interview today. The tubes are running, and King's Cross Station. I'll get home first thing if I can.'

'Well, I think you're *marvellous*,' said Nell, loosening up. 'Just marvellous. Never been to London before. And your accent's just like your poor mother. And ham!'

She led him down basement steps and opened a door. Facing them was a blast wall of stone slabs and walking round it – Nell led on – four people sat silent at a high iron table. Before each of them on the bare metal were knife, fork and spoon, and place settings for two more. There was a jug of water and four glasses reflecting the black surface, and a light hung down under a shade of ruched silk, once in a better room than this old staff kitchen. At one chair sat a petulant little bag of bones wiping her eyes and on the table in front of her stood a bottle of gin. The walls of the room were tobacco-coloured and, in the ceiling, gratings were covered over with oily brown paper criss-crossed with tape. With his back to an inner door sat a large and shambling old man, a pipe in his hand and a purple stain on his lower lip. One eyelid drooped. Even so, he had a certain air of bonhomie and the remnants of power. He was the retired dentist. Next to him sat the gin drinker and opposite them a man and a woman, staring at their knife and fork.

It was macabre.

'Yes,' said the man who was not the dentist. 'It's a Goya, isn't it?'

Jim Smith had not heard of Goya and thought that here was another, less-pleasant Jew calling him a goy.

'This is your Uncle Bob,' said Nell of the dentist. 'Well, perhaps he's your great-uncle. This is Cis. She has eye trouble. She's very ill. And these are Mr Shaw and Miss Gowland, our long-term lodgers.'

Nobody moved or spoke.

'Mr Shaw is retired from commerce and now works as a Fine Artist. Miss Gowland has been ever-employed by the Royal Mail in the local post office.'

The dentist cleared his throat and flung himself back in his chair. Cis sniffed hopelessly and pulled her shawl about her. Jim Smith noticed that there was nothing to eat on the iron table and that everyone looked desperately tired.

'Auntie Cis – here's Jim. *Jim*,' said Nelly. 'Betty's Jim from the north. He's going to be a doctor,' and Cis began to snivel quietly exactly at the moment the dentist bellowed out, 'Hullo, hullo. Hullo, young Jim. Glad you arrived safe. Greetings. Soon we'll go upstairs and listen to Churchill. Don't suppose you bother up where you live. It's nil desperandum here, old boy.' Then he seemed to implode upon himself and Auntie Cis sobbed out, 'I'm sorry. I can't talk. I've been so ill. I was never a well woman, never. Ask your mother.'

'I'm sorry. Yes, I will.'

'Betty's lot. You up there. You've no idea what we're going through down here.'

'Hush,' said Nell. 'There's been Coventry.'

'Mother said to say you're all very welcome to come north to us. She said she wrote it in her letter. She meant to come and *live*. But we're in the middle of airfields. It's not very safe. My school's being evacuated.'

Cis opened up her lace handkerchief and inspected it for auguries. 'We're finished, you know,' she said. 'They'll win. We're all as good as dead.'

'She's right,' said Mr Shaw. 'All this about our morale. Churchill – all he is is a warmonger, always was. An actor. This is Guernica here. On the flight path. We're finished.'

But the dentist was jovial. 'Come along, come along, what's all this? It's not over yet. They're not here yet. We'll fight them on the beaches and in the dentist's chair. A dentist is always king, boy. Right? I've enough gas in this house to fill a bunker. Have you plaque, boy, by the way? It's in the family. I'll see to it for you in the morning, if you like. Five shillings or near offer.'

Nell and Jim Smith sat down, and all sat on. On and on. Someone poured a glass of water. Jim Smith asked if he could use a telephone to ring his mother. If they had one.

'Oh yes, we *have* one. But you can't ring now, I'm afraid. The next raid will be starting in a minute. You'd have to hold on for an hour to get connected. And you'd be monop-olising the line. Sorry, boy.'

Jim Smith ached with hunger. He had not eaten since early

morning. There had been nothing on the train. Someone —
a pretty woman – had offered him a marmite and bread sand-
wich but he hadn't taken it. He thought of the ham in his
case in the hall and asked if he could wash somewhere but
was shown a cupboard place under the stairs: the old servants'
lavatory.

I could eat the soap, he thought, but there was no soap.
He was almost hallucinating as he tottered back to the table,
where they all still sat. I am among the dead, he thought,
the uncaring dead. Or I am part of a seance. Or I was killed
on the Underground and I'm in hell.

The door behind the dentist all at once banged open and
a cloud of warmth flooded in with a glorious smell of cooking
and a goddess filled the doorway. She bore a big blue oval
cooking pot. She was tall and blonde. A figure of gold.

Composed as Venus, she carried the casserole dish towards
the dentist and set it before him, retired and returned with
two big vegetable dishes. She removed lids and the dishes
were brim-full of steaming potatoes, carrots and greens. She
handed round heaped-up plates as Jim Smith gazed at her.
And gazed.

The goddess was old. She might even have been thirty.
She looked at nobody, half smiling to herself.

'This is the most wonderful, wonderful food,' he said.

Nobody spoke. The goddess returned to the kitchen. Cis
messed with her fork and sipped her gin.

The dentist preened. 'Yes, we didn't do too badly finding
Mac,' he said. 'Can't remember how she found us, as a matter
of fact. "Mac" she's called. Scotch lady. Second sight and

all that. Knows everything. Always gets the washing-up done before the raid starts. Can't believe our luck. Plenty of room here, of course, for her to lead her own private life and no questions asked. Child around, of course.'

'She looks, well, sort of Germanic.'

'Germanic? No. Couldn't have that. We don't ask questions though. The thing we like is that neither does she. She knows her place.'

In moments all the food was gone. Bulldog Miss Gowland leaned across to take the remains of Cissie's. Mr Shaw belched. Nell rang a bell that stood on the iron table. It was a brass lady in a crinoline and rang beneath her skirts. The goddess re-entered and stood looking intently at Jim Smith, who stood up in a trance and helped clear the dishes. Nobody else moved.

In the kitchen, among clean cooking pots and saucepans, sat a little girl about four years old, eating a slice of bread and margarine. Her eyes were as blue and her hair as gold and curly as her mother's. Mac stood by the stove, untying a hot wet cloth from round a dripping basin. She turned the basin upside down over a serving dish and lifted it away from a shiny suet pudding that oozed with sticky golden apples and the child stared and stretched an arm towards it. The goddess pushed away the small hand with her own that held a knife and cut the pudding into six exact slices, and the child went back to her bread and marg.

'Mac!' cried the dentist. 'Bravo! Whatever would we do without you!'

'They're our own apples from the back garden,' said Cis.

'Yes – but the suet! Where does she get the suet?'

'I wonder what she gives the butcher?' said Miss Gowland, speaking for the first time.

'I suppose there's no custard?' asked Mr Shaw, the Fine Artist.

'I'll go and see,' said Jim Smith, and picked up his plate and its helping of pudding, carried it to the kitchen and set it before the child.

'They are wanting custard,' he told the goddess.

'No. There is no custard.'

The child sat staring amazed at her slice of pudding.

'I don't like pudding,' lied Jim Smith and the child smiled. He went back to the dining room where conversation suddenly halted.

'Sorry,' said Jim Smith. 'I'm allergic to suet.'

Nobody asked what had happened to his plate but Cissie, sipping from a topped-up glass, said, 'She has no ration book, you know. Not one we have ever seen. Neither mother nor daughter. The child's not registered for orange juice. We took them in from the goodness of our hearts. I'm ill, you see.'

'Where's the little girl's father?'

'Ah, well,' said the dentist, leering, 'we ask no questions. And she knows her place.' Miss Gowland was licking her spoon with a fat, pale tongue.

'They don't sleep in the house now,' said Nell. 'Not since the raids began. They go up to the shelter on the Common. Well, it's none of our business.'

'There's something she doesn't care for here,' said Mr Shaw.

'That's why you're having her room tonight,' said Nell. 'That, and because Cissie's so much better, of course. Tonight we all sleep at Hilly Mead in our beds.'

'Or in the cage,' said Mr Shaw, patting the table top. 'The Morrison. I'm for the cage.'

'There's more to fall on you in a basement,' said Cis.

The goddess and her child now appeared at the kitchen door, Mac carrying bed rolls, a bag and a foreign-looking rag doll. The child clutched at her mother's skirt. Mac surveyed the black table.

'Wonderful dinner, Mac!' said the dentist. 'Wonderful, yet again. Good girl.'

'We are leaving for the shelter now,' said Mac, 'but I need help. I am unable to hold her hand while I'm carrying bed rolls.'

'I'll carry them.' Jim Smith was on his feet.

'More sense for you to stay here,' said Nell.

'Mr Shaw?' Mr Shaw did not move.

'You can't go, Jim. You won't find your way back. What would your mother think of us? They'll be here any minute now. We're right on the flight path in Wimbledon. To the city. We've a very high death rate here but it's kept quiet. We're not much safer than the East End.'

'Yes, you'd have done better where you came from, round St Paul's,' Miss Gowland volunteered.

The air-raid sirens began.

Fat Miss Gowland slid off her chair and down inside the table cage, and Mr Shaw joined her at once. Auntie Cis sat frozen and stared at the dentist, who took her hand and said, 'Cis – down we go. Or up. Whichever you want.'

'Come,' said the goddess to Jim Smith, 'take the bed rolls,' and she lifted the child in her arms and left the room. Jim followed up the basement steps, Nell running behind him with a tin hat.

'Take this. Put it on. Where's your gas mask?'

Mac was striding ahead up the hill in full moonlight and the child's bright face over her shoulder staring back at Jim.

'Your mother will never –'

'Come with us,' said Jim all at once. 'Come with us Auntie Nelly.'

But she said, 'Oh, I couldn't. They'd never forgive me. I hate quarrels,' and shut the door.

He followed the whiteness of the woman and her child up the hill until the houses stopped and darkness spread before them like the sea. They stepped into it and came to a door with a sloping back standing all by itself like a cupboard on the grass, and inside a steep cement stair disappearing into the earth. On the stair the smell of earth and grass gave way to the smell of urine. At the foot of the steps they batted against a blast curtain and a double brick passage, and inside were row upon row of people sitting quietly, one or two reading, one or two busy with a rosary, many sleeping for they'd been here for hours to get a good place.

Mac was greeted, space was made, the child was taken and embraced. The bed rolls were spread.

'Stay here,' said Mac to Jim Smith. 'Soon you will be warm. Here, take her,' and she lifted the child into his arms.

Her hair was sweet and clean and soft, and she leaned against his shoulder and closed her eyes.

'Here,' said the goddess again and passed him a flask with brandy in it. Then she drank some herself. 'The raid will be a long one tonight.'

'How do you know?'

'I know.'

It grew quiet. Only a few grunts and mumblings from the sleepers. 'Listen,' she said and, even so, very far below he heard the heavy, steady drone of planes.

'I'm cold,' said the child and the three lay down close together. The droning went on and on, a sickening lulling. Then, far, far above along the elected flight path the bombs began to fall – and fall – upon the suburban streets, along the railway, along the bending river, upon the palaces and slums and churches and hospitals and prisons of the city. Even down here, buried beneath the coarse green grass, the muffled juddering shook the humped and mostly brave backs of the people waiting.

'Lie here with us,' said Mac and drew the boy close to her with her child, and in the end, long, long after, morning came.

But there was no morning for those at Hilly Mead.

The Milly Ming

'I hope you don't mind my asking,' said Mrs Stott (we talked like this then: it was the sixties, in the suburbs and Mrs Stott was a Churches' Parish Visitor), 'but we have to make sure. This is a tricky little job. You aren't pregnant, are you, Mrs Ainsley?'

'You flatter me,' I said. 'I'm forty-five.'

'Good. And why are you volunteering?'

'I heard you needed drivers.'

'And you are a *good* driver?'

'I am. I drove my children to school for years.'

'And other people's children?'

'Yes. It was called the School Run.'

I was beginning to get annoyed. There had been a pencil on a string in the church porch and a notice saying 'Volunteers wanted for Amelia Menzies Babies. Occasional drivers needed. Sign here.'

Amelia Menzies had been a Victorian spinster living in a large house on the Common and looking after her father, a retired clergyman. When he died she went travelling abroad for a time and came home only to die shortly afterwards herself. She had left the house and its enormous grounds and a lot of money to set up a Home for unmarried mothers. It had been a sensational idea at the time.

At first the girls were the ones who wanted to hide away

or whose parents wanted them hidden away. They came to the Home only for the last months of their pregnancy. They were well fed and cared for, went to the local hospital for the birth, came back to the Home briefly afterwards. All was free and the Amelia Menzies Trust saw to it that they had funds to start a new life. The Amelia Menzies (we all called it the Milly Ming) was amazingly liberal. There was nothing said about penitence, only a recommendation that the girls attend church with the matron on Sundays and a firm rule that the coming child must be their first. A second illegitimate baby was not to be thought of. While at the Milly Ming, visits from outside were not allowed either. The girls had to come from places at least twenty miles away. Amazingly, when I arrived half a century on, the system was still in place.

I first noticed the girls when I came to the parish rather an outsider myself, for I had just gone through a divorce. I went to church alone and sat at the back, and I was a bit surprised during the first hymn when a string of heavily pregnant women filed in and settled in the pew across the aisle. I remember noticing that there was a Green Man carved on a pillar above their heads, leering down at them. Outside – it was a hot day and the church door stood open – you could hear radios playing all down the street: the Beatles singing about love. The girls shuffled out during the final hymn and didn't stay for coffee.

Adoption was the big recommendation at the Milly Ming, though I could never find out what Amelia had thought of it. Mrs Stott believed in it utterly. 'The ones who are hard to convince, of course,' she said, 'are the ones who are hardly more than babies themselves. No job, no roof, no family. But they don't understand. You have to *show* them that it is *better* for the child. It will have a settled family and a good education. And the childless have their rights, too. Up to now we've been very successful at persuasion but – I don't know – things are changing. They often want to keep the baby now. It's the Caribbeans all floating in. They believe in extended families.'

My job was to take the mothers who had been persuaded, sometimes two together, which Mrs Stott said was always easier, with their babies to the Adoption Centre. It was in central London and she warned me that it could be upsetting. 'They dress them up, you know, the babies, in the most incredible clothes. I don't know where they get the money, some of them. We take them up into a waiting room and after a few minutes a very nice, experienced woman comes in and says, "Here we are then. Off we go. Give her a kiss," and takes the baby away. And that's it.'

'And then?'

'Well, the adopting parents are very happy and excited, of course, across the corridor – door tight shut – in another room and do you know, the first thing they always do is take off all the clothes and dress the baby in other ones they've brought with them. It's quite wasteful really. Of course *we* don't see any of that. Our job is the girls. I'll always come with you. It'll be me or the vicar.'

'The vicar?'

'Yes. It's in the Milly Ming Trust documents. I often wonder if Amelia Menzies was a bit mischievous. I've never met a vicar yet who enjoyed it. It's a pity there are no *women* clergy, I say. There may be one day. You never know.'

The first time I drove to the Centre I sat outside in the car in the parking space that the police always left for us and it seemed a long wait. When Mrs Stott brought the now child-less mothers back at last they looked rather dazed. We asked them where they wanted to be driven but they said they'd get a bus and we passed them soon, standing at a bus stop, giggling and lighting cigarettes. They had pinched faces and heavy breasts.

'Don't fret,' said Mrs Stott. 'They'll have another one next year. Here's a tissue.'

'I think they're brave,' I said, 'brave not to have had an abortion. Brave altogether.'

'They probably never got round to having an abortion,' she said. 'More to the point, why didn't they use the pill?'

By the end of the sixties things began to change among the clientele of the Milly Ming. The girls complained that they couldn't have their boyfriends round, or go down the pub or out shopping. They were often aggressive and shouted and fought and walked out. There were some feminists. Numbers fell and there was talk of topping up the Home with the home-less, or even with hip-replacements-in-waiting. The staff deteriorated and the grounds were neglected. The matron gave up evening prayers. The church pew emptied.

The Milly Ming

One wet and vacant afternoon I walked across the Common to the Milly Ming to introduce myself as usual to the next mother I was to take to the Adoption Centre. I rang the bell long and hard before someone, bleared with sleep and in bedroom slippers, opened the door and flopped away. In the hall the Reverend Menzies's old crucifix was hung with coats. Facing it was the portrait of Amelia seated under a palm tree in the days of her foreign travels. She looked, as ever, a bright defiant woman.

I walked into what was still called the morning room, which was almost bare though there was a little writing desk I hadn't seen before and a perky-looking woman sitting at it. She didn't look up. But then both she and the desk were gone and there was only the drab room with the table-tennis table with its broken net.

A trick of the light.

A stately Jamaican girl, very near her time, was resting her forehead against the glass of a french window, watching the rain. She turned and said, 'So?'

I said I was to be her driver.

'Why they always send us *old* women?'

'Look,' she said, 'you wanna know something? I don't need no driver. I don't want no preparations. All I want is *out*. It out and me out. It's goin' to a better life – right? I know. I've had two already only don't tell them here. The first one thinks I'm her big sister. Fine. The second one she likes my mother best and my mother likes her best. Fine. So this one I'm dumping. Right? Old woman?'

'I see.'

'And it's going in a blanket. Right? And afterwards I'm going buying shoes.'

'I see.'

'Red stilettos. Don't look at me like that. Old woman.'

So then I left the morning room and made for the front door across the hall; but as I passed the portrait whose wide eyes were as usual gazing up the staircase behind me, I turned to look in the same direction and again I saw the woman who had been at the writing desk. Now she was standing looking down at me from the landing, the light behind her. Then she flicked away and there was nothing.

The Jamaican girl's voice made me jump and when I turned I saw that she was looking up the staircase too. 'Was she there again?' she said.

'Yes. Who is she?'

'She a ghost.'

'Is she a . . . happy ghost? She somehow looks a sort of . . . sort of a confident ghost?'

'Sometimes no. Sometimes she been a very *un*happy ghost. Jamaicans know about ghosts. At night she walk about, up and down, up and down. One time bad thing happen to her, I guess.'

'Are you . . . are you afraid here?'

She turned to look at the painting and said, 'Look. She in Jamaica there, see. She at Duns River Falls. She happy there, see.'

'I wonder why she came home?'

'I certainly do wonder that. Jesus, Joseph and Mary, I do wonder that!'

There was nobody now on the stairs but I think we were both listening to the silence.

'Won't be long. I'll see you again soon,' I said. 'I'm going home now.'

'You know then, old woman, what's home?'

The day came and Mrs Stott had the flu, and the vicar would be coming with us to the Centre instead of her. Could I manage?

I said, 'This girl's not friendly. All she wants is shoes.'

'There you are then,' said Mrs Stott. 'You'll all be fine.'

But we weren't.

Here on the appointed day was the mother, glorious in a low-cut dress in the hallway of the Milly Ming, and between the crucifix and the portrait the baby in a blanket lay on the floor. And here was the vicar, painfully young and blushing and very good-looking, and the girl couldn't take her eyes off him. 'Here,' she said and handed him the bundle. 'Now then, hand him down to me here in the back. D'you want to get in the back of the car with me, Reverend?'

But the vicar strapped himself firmly in the front of the car beside me. He was nervous.

Off we went on the long stop-start journey through the suburbs. And through the fumes of diesel from the road outside I began to notice the other smell in the car: fresh and milky and sweet, the smell of a newborn child. It is said to be the same as the smell of new-baked bread. It clutched at my heart.

So long ago.

'Why you cryin', old lady?' came from the back.

'Remembering my own.'

'That be some time ago, girl!'

She fell silent.

We arrived. We all sat silent, staring ahead.

Then the vicar found that he couldn't undo his seat belt. He said that he never could get on with other people's seat belts. He grew angry, and I had to bend and struggle with it down near the vicar's thigh, and he began to squirm and clear his throat, and I found that I couldn't undo it either. We began to bicker.

I bickered with the vicar.

And suddenly the girl in the back shouted – she *bellowed* out – 'Jesus, Mary and Joseph! I've had enough. Old virgins! I'm off. The shoes can wait. We're off home.'

I jumped out of the car, but she was gone with the bundle. The summer crowds passed up and down the pavement, and the world continued on its way.

I *am* an old woman now. I live in one of the twelve houses built over the garden of the Milly Ming, which still survives as six enormous luxury apartments. My arthritis is bad for I am almost ninety but I can look after myself and still cut my bit of lawn. Close under the hedge one day I found a tiny marble slab with some initials on it and 1899, the year she came home from Jamaica. Of course it may only be a pet cat: but I put flowers on it at Christmas and Easter.

The Hair of the Dog

The Airedale's head fitted snugly into the palm of her hand. The walking stick had been her husband's favourite, a present from their daughter Rosie, a very expensive present from the Burlington Arcade, bought over thirty years ago. Eleanor held the knob tight as she felt about with the ferrule of the stick on the station platform to step off the train. She took her time.

Then she thought, I must watch out. I'm behaving like an old woman on a stick. I could easily do without one.

But the dog's tiny ivory head was a comfort: a reminder of poor George's firm hand.

Victoria Station. She hadn't seen it in years. It was scarcely recognisable as the placid airy forecourt to the line of trains where, when she was young, she had waited for friends. ('I'll be under the clock. Don't hurry. I'll have a book.') There had been two trains an hour from Brighton, then, and in the nicest of them, the Brighton Belle, the rose-coloured lamps on the tablecloths in the buffet car had always been lit.

Eleanor was not what you'd call old, but she could remember steam. Perhaps even Rosie could remember steam, for Eleanor had taken her when she was small to see the last steam train out of Victoria. They had stood on the bridge at South Wimbledon to watch it vanish beneath them in its cloud of thin air.

Leaning on the stick, Eleanor watched the station now. The clock, hanging like a white full moon, was not there. There were no unhurried girls reading books. Everything was movement. Strings and streams of alien life all looking angry, resentful or sad. Or driven. People moved at a trot, never touching, never colliding. Sometimes they swept along in groups across invisible currents, confident, unstoppable: like bats from caves at sunset. She stood for a moment gripping the stick, closed her eyes, opened them and stepped into the mêlée.

She was on her way to lunch at the Goring Hotel, which she remembered as being just round the corner from the station, but now that she had reached the Victoria Street entrance, which was just the same (she remembered all at once that she had once stood here asking people to sign a petition against the execution of Ruth Ellis, the last – please God – hanging in England in 1955), now that she was here on the corner the Goring was nowhere to be seen. Maybe it was to the right, on Buckingham Palace Road. Somewhere around Grosvenor Gardens? This part of London had been her home once and she remembered its street names better than those in Wimbledon where they had moved next, and where Rosie had grown up and been married, and certainly better than the streets in Brighton where she lived alone now. In her mind she could see the white steps and polished brass of the Goring. She knew it still existed because a table had been booked there for this lunch.

So she would have to get a taxi. And the cab driver would

say, 'It's not worth the fare, love, it's just round the corner.' Then she would have to flourish the Airedale stick and look lame.

She stood for a long time in the taxi queue (thank goodness she'd come on the earlier train) and eventually it was her turn and the cab driver said, 'It's not worth the fare, love. Just over the road at the lights. Up left and turn right.'

So she walked to the corner and watched the skeins of traffic run by, and looked across to the memorial to Marshal Foch on his horse with the elegant tail. She had pushed Rosie in her pram to see him every afternoon. Now, the traffic screamed and streamed.

And there fell one of the mysterious silences that occasionally drop over London: the lull, the pause that happens in no other capital city (George had always said it was to do with the alignment of traffic lights) and that she had forgotten. Tears filled her eyes with the beauty of the silence, its promise. London froze.

But no, it did not freeze. It warmed. The poisonous air around Eleanor warmed and a cleansing waft drifted towards her, from the park and the wide streets of Belgravia to the north, caressing her hair.

Then it passed and the clamour returned, the crowds were all at it again, the police sirens and the ambulances. She took a hold on her mind and on the Airedale's head, turned from the traffic that pawed the ground behind the red lights and instead of right crossed left into Ebury Street where she had come as a bride.

For two pounds a week they had lived in a couple of

rooms above a maker of sculptured memorials and an angel, six foot high, had stared from his window each evening as she came home from the office. Its stone gaze knew when she was first home, which was almost always. It knew that she would have to go out again to buy the supper and that she had less than five shillings. 'And after that,' it said, 'when you are back with the sausages the phone will ring and you must be prepared for him to say, "I'm afraid I'll be late. Don't wait for me."'

The delicate eighteenth-century house, the whole of the long, eighteenth-century street, had disappeared with the angel long ago to be replaced by this blood-red stretch of four-storey mansions where a one-room apartment cost a quarter of a million pounds.

But north of it – away she went now, up Eccleston Street and into Belgrave Place and beyond – there were still the magnificent crescents and mansions that her daughter Rosie had beheld for her first two years, enthroned in her Silver Cross perambulator. Eleanor walked towards Grosvenor Crescent and here was a mews, each garage and pastel-painted little house breathing money. Burglar alarms decorated every one of the garrets of the nineteenth-century stable boys, and a chauffeur was grooming a thoroughbred Porsche.

'Yes? Can I help you?'

She said, 'I knew it here once. There was a little hairdresser,' and he turned away and went on polishing.

'Oh, but there's the flower stall,' she said aloud on the corner of Belgrave Square. 'Still blazing away.' And with suddenly young feet and the memory of her first high-heeled

London boots, her Mary Quant minidress and a particular hat – a silky sou'wester patterned like a Dalmatian – she plunged out in elderly brogues into the almost certain death of the traffic spinning up to Hyde Park Corner, flourishing the Airedale stick on high.

She reached the farther shore and paused on her stick beside the Artillery Memorial's bronze figures: private soldiers deep in thought, heads gravely bowed, a fourth lying dead, his tin hat on his chest. Survivors of 1914–18. Eleaner knew them well. She had over the years, when you still drove into London by car, stopped beside them stuck in traffic for ten minutes at a time. She was a pacifist and had regularly marched to Aldermaston but these four had always humbled her, exalted her: obedient, silent, unassailable heroes. They wouldn't have ended their lives tottering on fancy walking sticks.

She walked on, over the grass, past the ironic monument to Peace, carefully edged across the next flow of traffic into Green Park where she sat down on a seat facing the palisades of the garden walls of Buckingham Palace.

Around her, lovers lay in the grass like peasants in a Bruegel meadow but showing more flesh. Among them people ate lunchtime baguettes with both hands. Above it all the sky was high and blue, as high and blue as on the February day just over twenty-five years ago when she had come up to London from the Wimbledon mansion (George's late nights in the office had paid off) to buy the hat for Rosie's wedding.

*

'We always say, you know,' said the assistant in the small Knightsbridge store much classier than Harrods, 'that the wedding hat should be chosen *after* the hairdo. I hope I'm not being intrusive.'

What a nice girl, thought Eleanor. I can't imagine Rosie saying she didn't want to be intrusive. This girl loves her mother. I know it. Oh, if —. This girl is not too clever and she goes home to see her mother every week. Oh —.

'Actually, I'm on my way to have my hair done now,' she said, touching her pearls and mentioning a famous name. 'I've decided to go to the top.'

'Have you heard of this one?' The girl produced a card. 'He doesn't advertise. It's entirely word of mouth, but royalty goes. You should ask for *Gideon*. He's wonderful with straight hair. He cuts mine.'

Sun shone down on the girl's razor-sharp cap of straight hair and Eleanor thanked her and said she would come back to choose the hat later. Then she walked and stood outside the salon where she had the appointment. It was on the curve of a Knightsbridge terrace near Sloane Street and she watched through the acreage of plate glass all the beautiful people reflected in half a hundred mirrors. The faces, chins on chests, were very young, and the hairdressers looked even younger, and were enamelled and glossed like dolls. Everyone looked the same: a box of soldiers. Weighty glass doors with golden doorknobs the size of dustbin lids swung to and fro, and each time they released a heavy scent and loud music into the street.

Eleanor turned away and walked off. She walked and

walked holding the card in her hand until at length she reached a cobbled mews. One of the shabby cottages had rosy lights like the Brighton Belle and shone on the sunny day through trails of ivy and a wandering vine. There was nothing to suggest hairdressing. It was a cross between a tea shop and an orchid house, and it was silent. She walked in – a jingling bell – and it was warm after the February streets. There were mirrors and basins but bookshelves and climbing plants too, and a sweet damp smell. No one was about.

'Hello?' she called. 'Gideon? I'm to ask for Gideon.'

A gaunt young man stood at a doorway. 'Hi?'

'I'm told', she said in her magistrate's voice, 'that you are good with straight hair. Are you Gideon?'

'I am and I am.'

'I'm the mother of a bride. Someone recommended – well, I thought of a perm, actually. At somewhere well known. But maybe it's time to give up straight hair and I'm in the wrong place. I'll be wearing a hat, of course, for the wedding.'

'No,' he said. 'That's out of the question. You will not be wearing a hat. And no bag. And no matching shoes. You are not your mother. Sit down.'

She sat before a looking-glass that showed a green cave under the sea. She saw several young men sliding about in it. They were behind her, watching her. 'I'm so sorry,' she said. 'This is a man's hairdresser. I'm the only woman. I didn't know. This is a barber's shop.'

'Certainly not,' he said and took a piece of her hair on each side of her head behind the ears and pulled it down hard in the tips of his fingers. 'You have a horrible provincial haircut.'

'I beg your –.'

Scissors appeared in his hand and he began to cut.

'Oh! I didn't mean *today*. I only came in to make an appointment. The wedding's not until April.'

'That leaves us hardly any time. Coffee?'

'We're all gay, of course, here,' he said.

'Oh, well, yes. I realise that,' she said, trying to sound advanced.

'Now,' he said, 'we'll shampoo you and blow-dry.'

Years ago, Eleanor had learned how to circumvent the final moment of the ritual of a coiffure, when the client is 'shown the back' above the ever-ageing neck. She always closed her eyes and said, 'Oh, lovely, thank you.'

'No – *look*!' said Gideon.

A huge-eyed woman with the neck of a sylphide sat before him.

'But my hair's all gone!'

'For the moment. I shall need to see you again in two weeks. Let me show you the back again – eyes wide.'

Her neck looked a child's. The ears were very neat and small. She was brought a glass of sherry and an enormous bill, and tottered off towards the Goring Hotel where a friend awaited her for lunch.

The friend shrieked. 'You look like a lesbian. Or a chartered accountant.'

'But, you see, Rosie will –.'

'No, Rosie will *not*. She will not like it at all. Mothers of brides have to be nondescript. Unembarrassing. Wisps under a hat and eye shadow, and maybe highlights. Like when they were little.'

'Rosie won't − .'

'Yes, she will. She'll hate you trying to look trendy. Upstage her.'

'Upstage *Rosie!*' cried Eleanor. 'She's always thought I was plain and so does Nicholas and all his family, but she doesn't want me different and I'm not. I've simply had a haircut.'

'Eleanor, sorry, but wherever *did* you have your hair cut?'

'Oh, just somewhere I found in a mews.'

'Well, don't ever go back!'

But three weeks later she rang for another appointment. Gideon was even thinner, his eyes more hectic. Drugs, she thought, and watched his hands. But they were steady. He sat her down in a corner among potted palms.

'It's very hot in here,' she said.

'Yes. Torrid. Look out for the orang-utang. You look so pretty he might eat you.'

If this were my son, she thought, how would I feel? So thin. If this were my lover −.

'You are blushing,' he said and she said, 'It's the jungle.'

He picked at her hair like a monkey and meditated. 'We'll give you a treatment,' he said.

Soon she lay flat on her back on a leather day bed, her hair soaking in warm oils. Shadowy men slid by, oblivious. Again there were no other customers. Music began to play.

Above her in the corners of a grubby glass roof-light she could see the undersides of pigeons' pale starry claws. Her head at length was wrapped in a warm towel.

'OK?'

'I feel', she said, 'no guilt.'

'Whatever you on about?'

'This is pure, pure self-indulgence.'

'About time,' he said. 'There's no point in guilt. Too near remorse. Remorse kills,' and he began to tell stories about his clients.

'Where are they all, these clients?'

'Oh, they come here after five o'clock mostly.'

And he told her outrageous stories about weddings.

'Do you get on?' asked Gideon on the next visit.

'Who?'

'You and the daughter.'

Silence.

'Oh, well, you know *brides*,' she said in one of her false voices. 'They're all awful to their mothers, so I'm told.'

'How long has she been living with him?' asked Gideon.

'Oh, she still has her bedroom at home.' Then she said, 'Three years.'

'Did you mind? When she went to him? My mother did.'

'My husband minded. But she came home whenever they had "a break-up". As I've learned to say.'

'Sexy is she? Goes clubbing?'

'Oh, certainly not. She is a solicitor. She's very sensible. She plans her holidays a year ahead and her life is all arranged for the next twenty years. Actually, men – it's the same with all her friends – seem to be subsidiary.'

'God,' he said, 'I hate young girls. I like older women with nice houses and a couple of dogs.'

'That's conventional with you people,' she said.

'"*You* people"?'

'We have a cat. It's my husband's. And he has a walking stick with an Airedale's head.'

'Sounds kinky.'

He pulled on a suede jacket and walked with her down the road to the station. People noticed her shiny hair.

'Bye,' he said. 'Next time we'll dye it.'

'A few highlights?' she said.

'No. I mean *dye*.'

The days were warming. The big house was filling up with presents. The marquee people were being difficult. The caterers were all having babies and ringing up to say there would have to be substitutes. The garden, clipped and weeded to the bone, looked antiseptic. The gift from one of George's foreign clients – a van-load of green orchids – had disappeared into the entrails of Heathrow.

And Rosie the bride was missing too. George and Eleanor said they were forgetting her face.

'It's not asking much, Rosie. I'm not saying we *mind* doing it all alone but –.'

'I have to see Nicholas's mother, too, Ma,' she said. 'Don't forget she's a widow losing an only son. I have to be there a lot.'

'I sometimes wonder', said George in the background, stroking the cat, 'if Rosie ever thinks about us at all.'

'Your father wonders if you ever think about us at all.'

'But I *have* to help her with her bag and gloves, Ma. And the hat's so difficult.' She was on her mobile in Harrods, the mother-in-law-to-be chatting nearby.

The days began to breathe warmth into the April house. French windows stood wide open. In Rosie's childhood bedroom, two floors up, the wedding dress hung in its plastic cover from a curtain rail and rocked in the breeze. On one wall hung a long photograph of 500 clever girls at a famous school and Eleanor lingered to look at it. There was Rosie in the back row giggling beside her friend, Jacquetta. Already these girls had slipped into a time gone by; their dark tunics, white shirts, unpainted faces. Rosie and Jacquetta had the faces of laughing angels, of putti. They only needed little wings.

Oh – Jacquetta! Eleanor thought. Jacquetta had been like her own child. Jaquetta's hippy parents had been wandering India most of her schooldays on handfuls of rice and hash, while she had eaten toast and marmalade and crumpets and boiled eggs, and stayed with Rosie for term after term. Now Jacquetta was in Peru.

'Will there be bridesmaids?' Eleanor had asked Rosie at the beginning of all this.

'I'm too old,' said Rosie. 'My friends are all too old and their children are too young. Anyway, the only one I'd want would be Jacquetta and she wouldn't be seen dead.'

'But you haven't seen her in years.'

'She rang up the other day. She's back.'

'No! Did you see her?'

'No. I said I was getting married and she said bad luck. She's had a baby.'

'No! What? Jacquetta?'

'But it died.'

'Oh Rosie! Oh Rosie! What does she look like now?'

'How do I know? But she's coming to the wedding.'

'Oh, and by the way' – a week later and twelve days to go – 'Ma, Jacquetta does want to be a bridesmaid so we'll have to get her a dress. She's given me her measurements. She's broke. Green and white.'

Cash and tremendous cajoling had, through Eleanor's determination, produced Jacquetta's long green dress with white camisole and it hung like an iris from another curtain rail near the bridal gown, one on either side of the view of the silver birches below and across the room from the school photograph.

'My dress looks OK,' said Rosie. 'Very nice. So's your hair, Ma. Are you going somewhere new? Can I go there?'

'Will you do Rosie's and Jacquetta's hair?' she asked Gideon, who now knew every detail of Eleanor's life. He looked thinner than ever. 'Are you ill, Gideon?'

'No. Just have to be careful. Hepatitis. I try to keep fit. I'll do all the hair on the day. At your house. I never charge for wedding hair, by the way. It's one of my principles. I'll be there, let's see – wedding at two o'clock – I'll be there for breakfast.'

'You are so very kind,' she said. 'So embarrassingly kind. Why?'

'Because – oh, never mind. And you are beautiful.'

'Whatever is this?' said George when she reached home. 'Is this my wife? She burns on the water. She is the star of the silver screen. The marquee's holding up, by the way, and the orchids have arrived. They're green and white and I've filled the bathtubs with them. It seems a bit soon. Still forty-eight hours to go.'

'George,' she said, 'has Rosie phoned?'

'No. Of course not.'

'She was so quiet last time. George –.'

'She'll go through with it. Don't worry.'

'I think he's having doubts.'

'Oh, he'll turn up. He's a kind man.'

'*Kind!*' she said.

'Oh, Eleanor, she'll ring up at any moment. Hush.'

But when the phone rang it was Jacquetta. Jacquetta's familiar childhood voice but using a new vocabulary.

'*Jacquetta!* – Oh, darling Jacquetta! Rosie's not here yet. When do we see you?'

'On the day. Early morning. Hitching down through the night, yah?'

'Is that safe? Couldn't you come down with Rosie?'

'Not free. But I'll be there. No worries. Might even be the night before if I get a good lorry.'

'Lorry! Jacquetta, there's a hairdresser coming to do you and Rosie early. For free. He's marvellous.'

There was a gulp that might have been laughter. 'Going to be good,' she said. 'Ciao, Eleanor.'

On the Thursday evening Rosie telephoned in tears. She'd been to Gideon. She hated him. She hated the sleazy salon, she hated the hair. Nicholas was going to be livid. He would *never* get over it. It was all Eleanor's fault. She wept into her mobile not at all like a solicitor.

'Has this poofter insulted her?' asked George. 'Eleanor, he fancies you. Did you tell him that Rosie doesn't like us?'

'Don't! Don't say it. We never say it. We never face it. Oh, it's so bloody impossible being middle class. We're too *good*, George, too meticulous. Oh, George, I'd *never* have suggested it. She's not had her hair cut since she was eighteen. Oh, her wonderful long hair! Oh George – and it's gone. And Nicholas loved brushing it.'

'I don't care much for all that sort of thing,' said George, 'I'm afraid.' And he stroked the cat vigorously.

'Well, it's all over. There's nothing to be done. The wedding's a failure,' said Eleanor.

Old Auntie Dossie who had arrived early and was polishing some family candlesticks said that it would be a very pretty and happy wedding, and it must be difficult to be the mother of a bride.

*

Then, on the Friday, Rosie walked in with a huge bottle of scent for her mother, short golden curls and a glorious smile. 'Look at me! Nicholas loves it.'

'Oh!' cried Eleanor. 'Oh! He said he only did *straight* hair. However will we get the wreath on?'

'Are you *never* satisfied?' cried Rosie. 'And where's Jacquetta?'

'Tomorrow.'

'Oh, great. What's her dress like?'

'Wonderful.'

And that summer evening, twenty-five years ago, father, mother and daughter had sat eating shepherd's pie in the conservatory. Auntie Dossie and old Uncle Someone were somewhere indoors with trays. Everywhere about the Wimbledon mansion was perfect – cutlery, table linen, crates of champagne. Late daffodils shone in white clumps in the twilight. The marquee, like a grounded cloud, stood silver by the spinney under the white moon. Round the corner of the garden appeared Jacquetta, tall, skinny and totally bald.

George at once went out to her. Rosie shouted 'Hi!' and Eleanor fled.

George found her face-down upon the bed, gulping into the counterpane. 'She hates me! George – Jacquetta hates me. She hates me and Rosie hates me.'

'Get up at once!'

'*Shaven*,' wept Eleanor. 'I saw it gleaming. I saw her *pate*! Like the moon. It's her statement against us. Against all our suburban values. Did you see the gold safety pins through the lips?'

'Hush.'

'She'll flounce down the aisle, bald, drugged and pierced. Oh, why couldn't she have asked Julie Frobisher? Oh, and that lovely dress! And we paid for it.'

'This is beneath you, Eleanor.'

'Oh, I can't bear her being bald,' she sobbed.

Auntie Dossie called tremulously from the top-floor spare bedroom that the uncle had had a funny turn and was there any bicarbonate. Sitting beside the uncle's bed, Eleanor heard Rosie and Jacquetta in the garden talking hysterically like schoolgirls and falling over the guy ropes of the marquee.

'They're drunk,' she told George when he came in with Bisodol for the uncle.

'Oh, they always sounded drunk, the two of them, when they were together,' he said.

'That poor little bridesmaid,' said Auntie Dossie later on. 'How she's going to miss Rosie! She's the little friend who had the red topknot, isn't she?'

A cold, an icy shower engulfed Eleanor and she said, 'George. Come. Please.' And he followed her out of the uncle's sickroom.

'George. Do you think they are lesbians?'

He closed his eyes. 'No.'

'How can we know?'

'We do.'

'Should we tell Nicholas? Oh, she never sounds drunk with Nicholas. Oh – what do we know about our children? Not a thing after the first twitch in the womb.'

'Take a bath,' roared the father of the bride and thundered up to the top of the house where the girls now were. 'Rosie – the two of you. That's enough giggling. Your mother's going into the top-floor bathroom *now*. Right? The other baths are full of orchids.'

And Eleanor in the bath listened through the wall to the two girls talking. The talk murmured on and on between them and after a long time she heard their light being clicked off. The night before her wedding and her only daughter had not said goodnight to her.

'I must know,' she said, and in her dressing gown tapped on Rosie's bedroom door and went in. Jacquetta lay on a mattress on the floor under the window where the two dresses hung like flags in the moonlight. Rosie lay humped in her schoolgirl bed, moonlight on her new curls.

'Goodnight, you two,' said Eleanor, in her memsahib's voice. 'Don't talk all night.' She could not bring herself to kiss Jacquetta and was far too shy to give Rosie, who had fed for months from her breast, more than a peck. When she did make herself bend down to the moonlit face she found it wet with tears.

Early on the wedding morning a heat haze promised glory and Eleanor, walking in an old pink wrap, saw Gideon seated in the garden beside the conservatory, and there was something so unlikely and so comforting in his presence that she walked towards him and took his hands.

She opened her mouth to say, Oh Gideon! Something so terrible! The bridesmaid has a shaven head and studs all over her. We don't know –.

But she didn't. She remembered his wedding stories before the greenish mirror in the mews. The whisky priests. The ex-mistresses who ran weeping from the church. The lascivious mothers-in-law. She thought, And we will be the wedding where the bridesmaid turns up bald.

She went indoors with Gideon and he did her hair first. Then, since Rosie's and Jacquetta's room was still in darkness, he waylaid Auntie Dossie and turned her into Princess May of Teck. Then he made inroads into the uncle's moustache and eyebrows. George he did not approach.

Eleanor wandered off to the church through the garden gate and found it open and empty, and shining with orchids and sunlight. She said 'Thank you, God,' and wandered back again to find Rosie drinking champagne from a teacup in the company of a beauty with a red topknot. They were laughing. There were no gold studs.

'Jacquetta! It's lovely!'

'It's National Health,' said Jacquetta. 'I can't afford wigs from the likes of *him*.' She was laughing still, pointing at grinning Gideon.

'I'll fix it at the back, and the wreath,' said Gideon. 'Come on, there's not much time.'

'Too true,' said Jacquetta.

*

At two o'clock exactly, George, magnificent in ancient morning coat, reluctantly handing over his Airedale's head walking stick to an usher, led Rosie down the aisle to Nicholas and behind them walked Jacquetta. Two girls like tall flowers.

But at the reception Jacquetta was nowhere to be seen.

'Can't face it,' said Gideon. 'Can't face life without her Rosie. It's love, dear.' He swigged down champagne.

'You don't understand *anything*,' said Eleanor. 'Not one human thing. Except hair.'

'That's not nothing.'

'Oh no. Certainly it's not nothing. And thank you.'

The bride was changing into Armani jeans and nearly ready to leave. 'Where's Jacquetta?'

Eleanor stood about. 'She's flitted somewhere.'

Rosie looked intently out of the window. 'Oh, well, I'll see to her dress when I get back. Ma, I'll say goodbye to you here. Thanks for everything. Sorry you never liked me as much as Jacquetta.'

'Oh, *Rosie*! How can you! Oh, my Rosie.'

'And could you go in and water the plants at the flat?'

'You were crying last night,' said Eleanor. (A bellow rose up from the bridegroom in the hall: 'We'll miss the bloody plane.')

'Yes. It's Jacquetta.'

'What?'

'You saw her head. It's chemo. She's got about a year.'

*

'A wonderful, a perfect, a happy little wedding,' said Aunt Dossie. 'Now you and George go off by yourselves and I'll get Uncle into bed.'

George and Eleanor walked together in the garden, around the black mouth of the marquee. The odd white napkin lay in a flower bed, the odd wineglass glinted from the top of an urn. The daffodils whitened again as it grew dark.

Below the girls' bedroom window a long green tendril was caught in the branches of a silver birch tree and for a moment that seemed to submerge her whole life Eleanor thought it was Jacquetta's discarded body.

But it was only the empty dress.

And now, a quarter of a century on, Eleanor opened her eyes in Green Park, aware of an acrid, frowsty smell, and found that beside her on the long seat sat a tramp. He was deep in grime, head bent on chest, eyes turned up to her, mouth bloated. 'Can you give me forty pounds?'

'No, I can't,' she said and stood up.

'It's for my fare home to Reading.' He had a sack full of bottles.

She walked away, stepping among the lovers, consulting her watch.

'Oh dear, I'm late. And I was going to be so early. Oh dear, oh dear,' and she flagged down a taxi and said, 'Please, the Goring Hotel. I'm half an hour late for lunch.'

'Let him wait, dear,' said the driver and spun off towards the Mall. 'Love you all the more.'

She smiled and gazed at the crowds where nobody looked

as if they loved anybody. Nobody looked happy at all. Everybody was frantic.

For example, that woman standing beside Marshal Foch on the plinth. She looks as if she's going mad. Good heavens, it's Rosie!

'Stop!' cried Eleanor. 'Stop! It's my daughter. Can you toot at her?'

Rosie fell into the cab. '*Where* have you been? We've been waiting an hour. And they've done a silver wedding cake for pudding and all the children are here. And Jacquetta.'

'The grandchildren? Oh! Oh, that's wonderful.'

'Yes. It was to be a surprise. My silver wedding. Nicholas . . . And then you didn't turn up. We all met the train. We've been running the streets. All of us.'

'I took an earlier one.'

'Oh, Ma! Ma, Ma! Come on, quick. We can't start without you. Take care. Don't fall. Where's your stick?'

'I seem to have left it somewhere.'

'What, Pa's Airedale? Oh, no! Oh, Ma!'

'I'm afraid I fell asleep in Green Park. And – I think the Airedale may be in Reading. But I really don't need it at all. Not at all.'

'In *Reading*? You don't ever go to Reading.' (In Rosie's eyes, fear. Dementia. The first signs of the bitter end.)

'Ma, your memory is terrible.'

'No, dear. That's not true. It is certainly not true. Memory is a miracle. My memory is the best thing I have.'

Dangers

J ake was six and lived in America in the city of Boston where he had never seen a cow. Or a sheep. Or a waddling goose. Or a dazzle-coloured pheasant in the garden. (He had no garden.) Or a rabbit. Or a mole with tiny hands. Or hens scratching about and laying eggs and talking to each other in rusty voices.

Jake's granny lived in England down a country lane. Pheasants came marching through her garden. Rabbits hopped about in it. Cows loitered down past her gate four times a day, to and fro, to the milking shed. Sheep leaned against her fence, broke it down and ate her apple trees. The cows ate her blackcurrants and raspberries, stretching out their necks over the stone walls. When this happened Jake's granny went tearing out of her cottage flailing towels in the air. When Jake came on a visit, he thought it was very funny.

On Granny's birthday everyone went for a picnic by the river. The river was toffee-coloured with swirls of creamy bubbles rushing noisily in circles. Jake could not believe that he could just walk in up to his knees and play, and watch the fishes the size of needles examining his toes. When he wiggled his toes all the fishes turned together in the same direction and darted off in fright. Soon Jake began to make a great deal of noise in the river with a pretend gun.

Then Granny fell in the river.

Or, at any rate, she fell down the river bank, down on to the fat white pebbles. She fell sideways and downwards from a light canvas chair that had been placed not so much on the river bank as on what looked like a river bank but was really a web of tree roots covered in grass. Under the tree roots the river had scooped out a hole and round the sides of the hole was a honeycomb of rabbit holes. Granny had actually been sitting on air.

Bang, bang, bang went Jake's imaginary gun from the middle of the river. Sometimes he pointed the gun at Granny for fun. He pointed it at Granny and she fell slowly sideways down upon the stones.

'Dead?' called Jake in a nonchalant way.

Granny had hurt her finger and had to go to the doctor. Jake became quiet and that night cried when he went to bed.

He thought that he had tried to kill Granny.

'Of *course* not,' she said. 'It was an *imaginary* gun. Mind, you should never point a gun at anyone, ever, not even an imaginary gun.'

'I never will,' said Jake.

The next night it was pheasant for supper and he didn't like it. He had a tummy ache. Granny searched about in an old cupboard and found some arrowroot to tempt his appetite, which had been lost. He spat out the arrowroot and said that the pheasant was better than that. His mother and father said, 'You are being rude to Granny. Apologise.'

And Jake did. But that night he had dreams and said it was the poison.

'What poison?'

'The poison in the pheasant when they killed it.'

'Of *course* there was no poison. It was shot.'

'With a gun?'

'Yes.'

'Was it a real gun or an imaginary gun?'

'A real gun.'

'I will never *use* a real gun.'

'I agree with you,' said Granny.

The next day Granny and Jake went for a walk together along the lane. Jake couldn't believe a lane could be so empty of people and cars. 'I expect they're watching out for us,' he said from Granny's white wicket gate. 'I'd better take my rod.'

'Who's watching out for us?' asked Granny, nursing her finger, which had turned purple.

'The gunmen,' said Jake.

'Oh, come on,' said Granny. 'We're not pheasants.'

'I'll still take my rod.'

'Do you mean a fishing rod?'

'No, I'll catch fish with my pretend rod. This is just a rod,' and he went back into the cottage and rattled about in the umbrella stand where there were some mysterious things.

A shepherd's crook with bits of fluff in it.

Three tall walking sticks.

And a folded kite. A queer long branch with a 'v' at the end. You were supposed to hold tight to the 'v', one bit in each hand, and then the other end would twitch when you held it over invisible water, like a metal detector that doesn't twitch but screams. Jake knew you should try to have the water-finding stick with you whenever you are in a desert but as it was nearly always raining at Granny's – soaking, sparkling, lovely rain – the stick was seldom used. It was called a dowse.

'That's a dowse,' said Granny, 'not a rod.'

'No. This is what I have to take,' said Jake, burrowing about among thin sticks with little flags on them that other children had once run off with during a bike race. 'Here!' And he brought out a metal rod a metre long with orange plastic rings and a spike on one end. It was heavy.

'I don't like the look of that,' said Granny. 'I think we could do without it on this walk. It might go in someone's eye. Oh, all right then, but keep it pointing down.' They set off.

Soon the cows came thoughtfully along the lane. Jake jumped for the stone wall and flourished the rod. The cows stumbled a bit and swung away but on the whole decided that he was just being foolish.

'I'm protecting us,' he said and held the rod high, like a harpoon.

'I hate that thing,' said Granny. 'Wherever did we get it? Give it to me to carry.'

'I want to protect us.'

They came upon a heap of brown and green moss that

somebody had dumped under a red rowan tree. Jake prodded the heap with the rod. 'It's a dead cow,' he said. 'We don't have horrible things like that in America.'

'It is a heap of beautiful moss,' said Granny. 'Now give me the rod and we'll pick blackberries. See how perfect they are, black, red, pink, green, white.'

'They're full of seeds,' said Jake.

'Of course they are, but we only pick the ripe ones. We cook them with sugar and they're lovely with cream.'

'What is cream? We don't have cream in America, only ice cream.'

'You'll see. It's delicious. It comes from cows.'

'From cows? I think it wouldn't agree with me. You'd give me more horrible arrowroot.'

'Here,' said the exhausted Granny, 'my finger hurts. *You* can pick the blackberries. I wish you'd throw away that iron rod.'

'OK,' said Jake and suddenly did so. He flung the rod sideways so fast that it vanished like a needle-fish. It vanished through the stones of the field wall. It was gone in a second.

'Goodness!' said Granny. 'That was a quick decision. Had you had enough of it?'

'Oh, I'll get it back some time, I expect.'

They all ate blackberries and cream for dinner and Jake, after a few sips of the juice on the edge of the spoon, said they were very good and finished them up. 'I'll carry the bowl next time we go picking,' he said. 'I shan't mind not having the iron rod.'

'What iron rod?' asked Grandpa, walking in.

'Something he found in the stick stand,' said Jake's mother. 'I'm afraid it seems to have disappeared through a hole in a wall.'

'That would be the arrow we found,' said Grandpa, 'last year, lying in the stream at the foot of the ghyll near the waterfall. We couldn't think how it got there. It was a real archery arrow. A very dangerous thing.'

'Had it real feathers on it when you found it?' asked Jake. 'Like cowboys and Indians?'

'That is history,' said Grandpa. 'We've not had that sort of arrow in England for a long time.'

'Yes. There are none in Boston,' said Jake. 'It's quite dull there really, compared to here.'

Before he went home to America, Jake and Granny had another walk down the lane. The blackberries were over but the rowan trees still blazed red. Jake put an eye to various chinks along the stone wall but neither he nor Granny could remember exactly where they had been standing.

'I think it went right through the wall and swish, *pang*! Deep into the grass on the other side. Like in films. But I hope it didn't hit a sheep or a cow or a hen.'

'I think we'd have heard,' said Granny, holding her hand out to him and saying as she jumped him into the lane again, 'Not too tight now because of my finger.'

'I'm sorry about your finger.'

'It wasn't your fault.'

'Do you think my arrow will grow?' he asked, 'over the wall in the field? Will it grow an arrow root?'

'I expect something will grow,' she said, 'maybe a story. When you get home.'

Waiting for a Stranger

Lizzie Metcalfe leaned into the wind and took great plodding steps forwards and upwards to her line of washing blowing above the farmhouse on the fell. 'My, it's a tempest,' she said, opening her arms to the sheets that flung themselves against her, licked at her, enveloped her like living things. She batted them down, felt for the pegs along the line, somehow released them and gathered the whole great blossom of washing against her wide chest. Bending to the clothes basket, which she anchored with her foot, she toppled everything in and was almost blown away, down into the river valley.

'I don't know when there's *been* such a storm,' she said. 'End of October. Hot and wild. Winter next.' Holding the basket against herself she looked down past the farm, far, far down to where the river wound out of sight eastwards between bands of trees.

The trees were thinning. 'You can see traffic through the trees already.'

A car glittered for a moment along the banks. 'Like winter.'

The glitter came again, now rather nearer, and the car like a bright bead shot out of the trees and turned towards the bridge and Lizzie's side of the river. 'Here he comes, then,' she said. 'Why couldn't he have said whatever it is he has to say on the phone?'

The car disappeared into another fold in the land beside the water meadows. Invisibly it would now be climbing up beside the ghyll and the fosse. By, and that'll be a spate today, she thought, with all the torrents we've had, and the trees tossing.

She pressed forward into the house, dumped the washing basket on the table, calculated the time she had before the car arrived and decided there was just enough of it to shake out the sheets and put them in the back-boiler house for airing. Cars had to stop at the foot of the home field, which was too steep for anything but a tractor. You walked the final bit. She went outside again, shading her eyes with her hand. The car, busy and bright, was turning the last bend, plunging under the two sweeping larches. 'Kettle,' she said, went back in, filled the electric jug, switched it on. She looked in the mirror at her wild hair and glowing face. 'I'll do,' she said. 'Anyway, I'll do for the minister.'

A knock at the door.

'Lizzie? Hullo. Jim Carritt. The minister.'

'I know,' she said, 'I've watched you from miles back. Kettle's on. Are you blown to bits? Come on in.'

'Nearly,' he said. 'A gale and a half. Hallowe'en weather.'

'That's tomorrow.'

Clouds crossed the sun. Doors banged about the farmhouse and there was a long tearing crash as some stone roof tiles fell from a byre on the yard.

'Don't you get frightened, up here alone?' (He thought, There's something odd up here today. As if there's sorrow coming.)

'Never,' she said. 'I'm not alone at night. There's Edward and the boy.'

'Are they far now?'

'No, down Dale. Working with sheep. They'll be back for their teas.'

'They should leave a dog up here with you.'

'Whatever harmful could come by?' she said. 'Sugar? Teacake?'

'No, thanks. Yes, please. You are a famous cook, Lizzie. Lizzie, I have something to ask you.'

'You said on the phone. But if it's the butterfly cakes, you've asked already. I'm making a hundred tomorrow. I'm bringing them down well in time for the Ecumenical. I'd not forget.'

'It's something else. Lizzie, I'm going to ask you to have one of the delegates. To the council. Coming to the cathedral.'

'Have?' she said. 'Delegate?'

'He's a bishop. An African. We've had people back off, and I'm left with this one bishop stranded. Would you have him?'

'High Place is no place for a bishop,' she said. 'There's no en suite here. Would it be just B&B?'

'And evening meal. I'd bring him and call for him first thing next morning. He won't want entertaining. He'll be just off his plane. And he's decided he wants to drive up straight from the airport, which will just about kill him, I'd think. He'll want early to bed.'

Lizzie sat down on the kitchen stool with her tea. She had forgotten to take the minister into the sitting room. People of his substance usually sat in one of its armchairs with the lace arm pieces.

'You have a spare room?'

'Oh yes, there's mother's. It's full of boxes. And her clothes. It takes time to get rid of the clothes, you know, but they'll have to go one day. It might force my hand.'

'Would it be a trouble?'

'No, no. I only have your cakes to make.'

'So you'll do it?'

'Well, I dare say. Will he be in robes? We're Chapel here, you know.'

'Well, I'm Chapel,' said the minister, 'in case you've forgotten. We're Ecumenical now. That's what this council is about. I'd think he would be very unlikely to be in robes on the motorway.'

'And I *suppose*', said Lizzie, 'that he'll be black?'

'Well, I'd think so. He's from Central Africa. Gurundi. I hope that doesn't worry you?'

'It gives me a funny feeling,' she said. 'I've never seen anybody black in the . . . in the flesh. Just on the telly.'

Another thought struck. 'Mr Carritt, is the reason you've had to come all the way up here to find him a bed because he's *black*?'

'No, no, of course not. Shall we say that some people are, well, just a bit shy. You know the Dales.'

'Oh, I know "shy",' she said. 'I've no time for "shy". They're happy to watch *Casualty*, aren't they, and *The Bill* and them funny London Indians taking the mike out of themselves and making you laugh like nobody. But when it comes to giving one of them a bed, it's "shy". Bring him here. I'll get his clean sheets on.'

'An African bishop?' said Edward later, in from sheep. 'Coming here? What'll we talk about?'

'Well, we'll talk about Chapel, can't we? And the Ecumenicals and the church and the choirs we're in.'

Their son, Alan, who was no talker, suddenly said that if the bishop was coming he'd not be there.

'Why not?'

'It'll be voodoo and that. I'll stick to my bedroom.'

'You'll do no such thing. You'll do as you're told.'

'I'm eighteen.'

'It's because he's black, isn't it? Yet you're mad for Venus Williams.'

'It's not that. It's because he won't like us, that's what. What can we be to him? We've never been anywhere and he's from Africa and driving himself up the A1, which none of us could do. He'll think we're primitives. He won't know what to mek of us. He'll tell them back home we're Neanderthals.'

All next day father and son dipped sheep while Lizzie cleared the spare bedroom, made a steak and kidney pie and a hundred butterfly cakes. The wind still roared. The house was still restless. At teatime the men blew in through the yard door to find Lizzie in the sitting room in her good dress. Just sitting. The waiting house seemed full of the storm. Ill at ease. There was no sign of the bishop.

'So where's His Eminence?'

The fire blew a mocking roll of smoke down the chimney and across the sitting room.

'This wind's nasty,' said Edward. 'Evil-tempered. It's Hallowe'en and it feels like it.'

'That's voodoo,' said Alan.

Lizzie remembered a Hallowe'en in her childhood when the cat had gone mad and run up the curtains, hissing at something that wasn't there. 'It's all right,' she said. 'The dogs are quiet.'

'So we'll have to wait for our tea?' asked Edward.

At seven Alan said he was taking his steak and kidney and a cake or two upstairs. Soon, occasionally, above the storm, sounds of his computer game could be heard.

At eight, Lizzie gave Edward his pie and rang the minister, but got only the answerphone. 'He'll be on his way,' she said. 'I'll wait up. He can't ring me from his car, mobiles not working up here.'

At ten Edward went up to bed and Lizzie rang the minister again with the same result.

She went upstairs and stood looking at the room she had prepared. Without her dead mother's belongings it seemed large and bare, the sheets very white; the two dahlias in the white jug she had put by the bed shone out.

African people like bright colours, she had thought.

She crossed to the window now and looked at the night. Only five pinheads of light showed down the Dale, two of them intermittent behind labouring branches. No stars.

There's an angry spirit abroad, she thought.

And then, What rubbish. Hallowe'en. All Souls. How can there ever be *all* souls wandering about? It's Papist.

On the stairs she said loudly to the dark, 'Anyway, tomorrow is All Saints. By midnight it will be All Saints.'

She sat now in the kitchen where the bishop's dinner was still keeping hot over a saucepan between two plates. 'He'll not come now,' she said, 'but I can't just go to bed. If they turned up and everything in darkness, it wouldn't do.' She slept as she sat, and much later woke and found that the wind had dropped and there was silence. A single cinder fell in the grate.

Her mother's wall clock struck twelve.

She found herself standing up and looking first at the clock and then towards the door. And after a moment, somebody knocked on it.

Never! she thought.

'*Never!*' she called, crossing the stone flags. '*Never!* Well, you poor soul! Wherever have you been? Is Mr Carritt there?'

On the doorstep stood a small, thoughtful black man in cassock, anorak and dog collar. He carried no luggage. He stood outlined against a pure, still night and a sea of stars.

'Bishop – oh, dear – come in. Where is Mr Carritt? However did you get here?'

'I am alone,' said the bishop. 'There has been a hitch, but I found my way. I understand that I am wanted here.'

'You are, you are –. But – the dogs didn't bark.'

'I am very fond of dogs.'

'You must be famished. I've kept you something hot. I'll make up the fire.'

The bishop looked around him. The saucepan. The regiment of cakes.

'You are so very kind. But I'm afraid I'm rather beyond eating.'

'Then I'll get you some tea.'

He looked at her and smiled, and she thought she had never seen anybody so calm and happy. 'I'll show you your room,' she said. 'The bathroom's along the passage.'

He looked kindly at the room, his dark face smiling at the dazzle of the sheets, the bright dahlias. 'No tea,' he said.

'There's a hot-water bottle in the bed,' she said.

'God bless you,' said he.

Climbing in next to Edward she thumped him. 'Edward – he's here. He's all alone. He's gone to bed,' but Edward was deep sunk in sleep as, in a moment, so was she.

And in the morning, not long after six, Edward and Alan already out milking, she was woken by the telephone shouting at her from the kitchen and stumbled down, half awake, without her dressing gown. A cool, bright day.

It was the minister. 'Lizzie, Lizzie – I'm so sorry!'

'Why?' Then she remembered. 'Oh, don't be sorry. It didn't matter. All was well. I don't know how, but he –.'

'Lizzie. Will you just sit down for a moment? I'm afraid – are you awake? Is this too early? I'm afraid I have some horrible news.'

'News?'

'The Bishop of Gurundi had a car crash last night on the

A1. Near Scotch Corner. Just after six o'clock. I went straight to him at Northallerton Hospital and I was with him until midnight.'

'Midnight?'

'Yes. And then . . . and then he died.'

Putting the phone down without a word, Lizzie went straight upstairs and knocked.

Then she went in and stood in her nightdress at the end of the bishop's bed. The white sheets were there, unslept in, and the light of a heavenly morning streamed in through the window.

There was not a soul there.

Learning to Fly

The vineyards filled the valley between the fluted mountains that already in the early morning seemed to float in heat. Here and there they parted to let a road through, encircle a village. At one point they gave way to an electric fence that surrounded a small country-house hotel. Inside the fence, Allie Vigne sat on a veranda watching the bad-tempered South African ibises strutting and shrieking as they plunged their curved beaks into the lawns. A hot wind had begun to blow and she sat dabbing the palms of her hands with a napkin as she waited for breakfast. She examined them. The black girl, Lily, with her baby under her arm, watched her from round the veranda door.

'You have your breakfast now, Mrs Vigne, or wait for Mr Vigne?'

'I'll have some coffee now.'

'You reading your palms now, Mrs Vigne?' Lily set the coffee on the table, the baby secure on her hip. He was young. Not able to sit up alone yet. He was beautiful.

Allie put her big white English hands on the table.

'You know how to read palms then, Mrs Vigne?'

'No. Oh, no. I've just read things about it in magazines.'

Lily and the baby went away, and Allie brought her hands up before her face again, looking at the familiar long straggling lifeline.

'Will you read my palm next, Mrs Vigne?' Lily asked, coming back suddenly with toast. 'Will you read the other girls' palms? Linda's going to have an operation. Will you read Friedrich's palm?'

'No, no.' But Lily stretched out a hand that held Friedrich's little pink and blue pad inside it. The baby's lifeline, head-line, heartline were all safely in place. 'Oh, how lovely,' said Allie and stroked the baby's palm with a finger. The baby laughed.

'Is he going to live a long time? Am I going to live a long time?' and Lily held out her own sweet plump hand, the smallest adult hand Allie had ever seen.

With the shortest lifeline. It stopped abruptly, not an inch long.

It's all nonsense, thought Allie.

'Yes,' she said, 'it looks as if you'll both live for ever.'

'How many babies will I have?'

Allie looked and said, 'Three.'

'Three? Then Friedrich is my last child.'

'You look much too young to have three children.'

'Yes, I am very young. And I am very strong. Your hands are very strong, Mrs Vigne, but my hands are stronger. Look.' She flattened out her hand, swung the baby from under her other arm, stood his tiny parcels of feet on it, let go of him and raised him, his legs straight, high in the air. He shouted with joy and Allie screamed.

'He'll fall! Stop! Oh, he'll fall on the tiles.'

The baby laughed. He stood almost on tiptoe. A diver

about to plunge, arms out gracefully sideways. A bird about to fly. 'Oh, Lily! Stop!'

'It's OK. Babies can. In my family. Easy, easy. They like it – look! My mother did it with me and her mother with her. We are learning to fly.' She bounced the baby up off her hand and caught him as he came down. They spun round together, laughing.

'*Never* do that again while I'm around,' said Allie.

It was the Vignes' last day of holiday and they drove up into the mountains to a small town where the streets were lined with lavender. Over lunch they noticed the scent of it was mixed with an angry burning smell that came up from the plain.

'It really is too hot,' said Allie. 'It's time we went home.'

They drove on and what seemed to be the whole Cape stretched below them, the miles of immaculate vineyards. Here and there smoke rolled across them, and on the way home they came on closed roads, police, fire engines, helicopters. They pressed the button on their hotel room keyring to get through the electric fence, showered and changed, and went out again to a restaurant in the city for dinner. The smoke on the plain behind them now seemed to be halfway up the mountains and on the way back Allie cried out, 'Look!'

The whole sky northwards was a wild red, and flames were running up and down the hills that seemed to have stepped much closer. As they drove up the dirt track to the electric gates animals sprinted out of the grasses. A huge owl with ears swung down. It sat watching, from a post. The automatic gates closed silently behind them.

'We couldn't get out', she said, 'if –. And we're alone tonight. The girls all sleep out on the farms.'

Her husband said he wasn't worried. 'Not unless the wind changes,' he said.

All night from their window Allie watched the flames rippling up and down the hills, blossoming crimson, sometimes miles apart. She believed that she could hear the roar.

She thought, Lily and the baby are somewhere out there.

And saw again the short lifeline on Lily's palm.

She fell asleep at the window and awoke stiff and late, her husband already packed for the plane, examining the airline tickets. 'You worry too much,' he said.

Downstairs in the kitchen they could hear the girls clinking dishes, laughing and talking with the babies.

'Oh, I was scared in the night,' said Allie to Lily on the veranda.

'Us, too,' said Lily, 'but it happens all the time. Just heat.'

'It's a dangerous country.'

'Oh yes, but please come back to it,' said Lily, 'and now please let us have a hug,' and holding Friedrich she hugged first Allie and then Allie's husband tight, laughing and crying.

'We may not meet again,' said Allie. 'Nobody knows the future. *Nobody* knows, Lily.'

'Yes, but look at Friedrich,' said Lily. 'Up, up he goes. Now don't be afraid, Mrs Vigne.'

And Friedrich spread his small arms sideways, stood up, straight in the air on his mother's little hand.

'Look at him, Mrs Vigne, look at him flying.'

The Virgins of Bruges

On the morning of Christmas Eve my sister's husband died. I live in Paris. She lives in Herne Bay. She telephoned me at once and at once I said that I would come.

'Of course you can't come.'

'I shall start now.'

'It's Christmas. You'll never get a seat on a plane from Paris.'

'Of course I will.'

'You won't. I've asked.'

She had already asked. She *did* want me.

But even if she had not wanted me I would have gone to her. Frédérique is unlike me. She is a mother, wife of a farmer, beautiful, resourceful, practical, intellectual. I am a small, short nun.

'I'll ring the airport,' I said. 'If there's really no hope, I'll try the Tunnel.'

'The Tunnel won't help, it would be worse than the airport. You'd have to go all the way up to London and then back down here to the coast again.'

'I'll try the ferry from Zeebrugge.'

'No, try Ostend. Ostend to Ramsgate. I'll meet you at Ramsgate. Ring me.'

'Oh, Frédérique. Oh, I don't believe it, now that it's happened.' It had been expected.

'Neither do I,' she said. '*Gentil*. Kind Ursule.'

We were at one again after years of distance. We are all that is left of our French family.

I took the first train possible to Ostend and late in the afternoon arrived there to stinging sleet and darkness, and to find that there would be no more cross-Channel ferries until Boxing Day.

'Zeebrugge? Calais?'

None. Not until Boxing Day.

It may be imagined what sort of people would be staying over Christmas alone in the cheapest hotel in Ostend. The one I was standing in echoed with concrete, and smelled of disinfectant and old booze. A desolate Belgian yawned at the desk. He was cleaning his nails with a biro. I looked at a room. Thin bedding, stained carpet, no bathroom, brown high shadowy walls. The smell of canals.

I took a bus into Bruges, the city of holy treasures, the city of Benedictine sisters behind their high walls, and of pretty bridges over swan-scattered water. The city of The Drop of the Holy Blood, of the Michelangelo Virgin sitting in her chapel so straight and young and wise.

My community had allowed me very little money for the journey, but surely I could find somewhere there to sleep. Then I would go to a midnight service.

Bruges is a short distance from Ostend. I stepped out of the bus with my suitcase and went searching. I had expected some sort of bustle of Christmas in Bruges and a barrage of bells. I did not know Belgium. Nothing perhaps had started yet? It was quiet. The snow fell, settling as slush, but it was growing colder. It was dark. I walked about the Steenstraat and along the Wollestraat, and at last I was directed to the south of the city and the holy sisters. I am not a Catholic nun and I don't wear a habit, but I wondered if nevertheless they might take me in. However, all was closed.

And so I walked over slabs and cobbles and paving stones and crossed several bridges over black water, and somewhere near the Street of the Blind Donkey I found a small hotel. It was too expensive, but I was tired and cold, and it seemed warm and comfortable. I stood for a long time at the desk ringing for attention until at last someone came out of an office where a television screamed. He did not seem over-joyed to see me and told me that they did not serve any food.

Might I telephone from my room to England?

He said there were no telephones in the rooms and I would do better to phone from a restaurant when I went out to dinner.

So after another walk in the snow I found a restaurant that was not too expensive. It was packed full of people smoking and shouting, but the food was hot and good, and they sat me in a quiet corner. I telephoned Frédérique from a phone on the wall and all she could say now was '*Gentil, gentil*', again and again and again. '*Gentil*, Ursule, *gentil*.'

Frank had been young. Not forty. A fruit farmer. He had orchards, which he had linked under the ground with pipes of running water. The trees were a glory in spring and in autumn, when I had occasionally been there to help pick;

spare apples stood in golden pyramids on the grass rides, swept together after harvest. Such riches. There had been fields of strawberries too, grown in trays like shop counters so that the pickers didn't have to bend down, and we had all stood at the counters, about forty of us, laughing and talking across the field and our fingers smelling of strawberry juice all the summer. Poor Frank marching by on his long legs. The children around.

I said to Frédérique, 'It's got to be Boxing Day. I'm so sorry,' and she said, 'But are you safe? Are you all right there?'

'I'm fine. Good hotel. Don't worry. I'm furious, but don't *worry*.'

'But weren't you needed in Paris? Look – you must go back.'

'Of course not.'

'But what'll you do? Tonight and tomorrow?'

'I'll go to bed early, or I may find a midnight service. It should be good in Bruges on Christmas Day. Don't meet me on Boxing Day. Have you a friend there?'

'Dozens if I want them, but I don't. I'll meet you at Ramsgate. Love you.'

She said 'Love you'. Frédérique!

So then I had coffee at the corner table and went back into the streets to look for a church. I did not want Notre Dame or famous St Saviour's. I wanted a quiet church in a side street. I didn't want roaring carols tonight.

Soon I found one. It was in a wide, silent street and loomed down at me from the top of a broad flight of stone stairs.

Down the stairs flowed a red carpet, presumably for Christmas. It was wet and dirty with snow. Here and there on the steps people were sitting in twos and threes, and one alone. They were mostly girls. I stepped round them up the steps, wondering why they were sitting out in the snow. When I reached the top step I turned and looked down at them. The girl sitting alone had fallen sideways. In the shop doorways across the street I could see other people standing in shadows, quite silent. Quite still.

Then one of the girls on the steps cried out and another one turned and looked up at me and began to laugh.

I was rather frightened and went quickly towards the church, where the high doors stood open and a man came forward out of the dark towards me and bowed. He was in evening dress and his hair was short and black and seemed painted on his head, like a harlequin. His face was blank. He stood inside the doors near a font at the top of the main aisle, and on either side of the font were two giant metal candelabras lit with hundreds of white candles blowing in the icy air. It looked as if a pilgrimage had just passed that way, but when I looked down the centre of the church, the pews were empty. Above them hung the shredded flags of old battles in two limp lines, as they must have hung for centuries.

But up in the chancel, which was as high and wide as a cathedral chancel, everything blazed crimson and gold and was crowded with people, and behind them, in all the niches for saints and bishops, there was nothing but the gleam of coloured glass. In front of these niches, stood a very long altar lit by more candles, though some had fallen over. Around it, on every side, people perched on high stools whispering and sniggering and embracing, and lolling like the people outside on the steps. And I thought, This must be some sort of Belgian Christmas pageant.

But the Last Supper is not to do with Christmas, even in a city dedicated to the Holy Blood.

Then I saw that the glass in the niches was made up of coloured bottles and there were more bottles on the altar, some of them on their sides, and that the people sitting round the altar were using it as a bar, and that most of them were either drunk or drugged and were resting their heads on the altar or embracing each other or stroking each other, and one or two of them were lying about lopsided on the chancel floor.

And it seemed to me that most of them had beaks or snouts, or claws and hoofs, and that their bodies were not the bodies of people but of eels and toads and serpents and leathery black lizards or blood-red scaly dragons, and that here and there was a horn and a tail.

And I fled out of the church (the nightclub now) and passed the people on the steps and in the doorways. The snow had stopped falling and the stars shone out and on the church steps I saw the glitter of a syringe, and then, at the bottom, someone in the gutter, and the people in the doorways watching. And I ran away down the street towards the hotel.

But I could not find the hotel.

In the starlight of the great square of the city, no one was to be seen. The snow was untrodden. I must have dreamt all this, and still be dreaming.

And so I began to pray that the dream would end.

And all at once the bells of Bruges began to boom and bang and throb and echo about across the city, and I realised that I was wet and cold and awake.

And I swear that what I have described to you is true.

Then from all the streets around people began to appear and doors began to open on to the snow, and voices began to call to other voices and black tracks were trailed across the snow as the people walked towards the churches. They passed me without a word or a nod. I felt that I could not follow them.

Instead, I turned and found myself going the way I had come, back towards the terrible things I'd seen, and I easily found the church with the sopped carpet down the steps, but the doors of the church were now shut.

I looked about and I couldn't see anyone in the doorways across the street. The girl with the syringe and the one who had laughed and all the rest were gone, except for the one girl, the one who was lying down all alone.

So I went up the steps to her. She was very young, in poor clothes. She wore no ring. She was pregnant. In the last month. I thought at first that she was dead, but when I touched her she was not dead. Her eyes opened, and she said in Flemish and then in French and then in English – it was very strange – 'Please help me to a hospital.'

I looked up the steps towards the church, then down to the street, and at first there was nothing. The bells of the city were stopping now, first one and then another, until there was just one left, dong-donging high and clear. And then that too ceased.

Then traffic seemed to start again somewhere and, almost self-consciously, a taxi came round the corner. It stopped for me, and I took the girl to the hospital and there I learned that Bruges is not entirely the city of Hieronymus Bosch.

And I waited in the hospital all night for the child to be born, which it was, on Christmas morning.

The Fledgling

Lester came wandering along the towpath in the moon-light feeling drunk, free and yet not altogether happy. It was late. He'd been playing music down the Painted Sailor on the quay. Tomorrow he was off to college.

At his back-garden door in the high wall he couldn't find his keys. Then he thought, It'll be open. They wouldn't have locked it.

The door was locked. Glancing up to consider whether to try to climb over the wall, he found himself looking into the eyes of a severe and magnificent mallard drake standing in the ivy.

'Hi,' said Lester. 'They've locked me out. "Behold, I stand at the door and knock." But they've locked me out. And I'm leaving tomorrow.'

He found his keys, dropped them on the gravel, fumbled about for them. 'You'd have thought', he said to the drake, 'that they might have wanted me to stay home the night before I left. Eh? Not a word. They might have stood me a meal. Most parents do. But no. Mallard, THEY DO NOT COMMUNICATE.'

He picked up the keys and found that the door in the garden wall had been open all the time.

The house was in total darkness.

'You would have *thought*,' he said – though the mallard

had disappeared — 'that they might have waited up. Well, I know it's not forever and I'm not going far; but look, I've lived with them *eighteen years*. They'd have had a *lodger* in for a drink the night before he left, after eighteen years.'

The back door was also unlocked and he went into the house and at once fell over a huge quantity of luggage piled up inside. What they doing with my stuff? This is my private property. *Two* suitcases! She must have been ironing shirts all day and she knows I don't wear shirts.

You can't talk to her. She was . . . my mother was . . . she was great once. Beautiful. And she thought I was wonderful. And my father was someone. He doesn't say a bloody word now. You'd think he was afraid of me.

'They're taking me, though,' he said. 'As if it was a boarding school. I've got mates there already and it's not fifty miles off, and I'm coming back often enough, but they're taking me. *And* he'll wear a suit. I know he'll be in a suit.'

On the landing he fell over a double bass.

'Am I taking that? Apparently not. They've left it up here. Oh God! Going to bed. Crash.'

Under the covers of the bed he had slept in since he was five years old, he wondered what bed he'd be in tomorrow night.

Some six hours later his mother, Stella, was woken by a tremendous pandemonium in the garden. Squawking. Crashing. The breaking of branches. A cacophony of ducks. 'It's ducks fighting,' she said and was at the bedroom window.

'Ducks aren't great fighters.' Her husband was lying straight in their bed, nose to the ceiling. 'They're sober birds.' He had been awake for some time.

'Well, there's something horrible going on,' she said. 'Oh God! I hope it's not that cat. Or the fox.'

'Why ducks?' said he.

'Well, for God's sake, Alec, they're *quacking*.'

'It is six in the morning,' said Alec. 'You are hanging out of the bedroom window in the dawn. Ducks are quacking. What do you expect ducks to do?'

'But we're –. We thought they'd never come back. Ducks used to come here. The same ducks, year after year. They told us so when we bought it.'

'I never believed all that stuff,' he said. 'It was estate agent's blurb. Ducks don't lay where there's no water to launch the ducklings. And this is October. No duck would be nesting in October.'

'Well, they're here,' said Stella, bringing her head in from outside the window. 'Maybe the climate's changed. Maybe they think it's still summer. Or they may just be late parents, like we were. Maybe they'll only produce one. Like us.'

'God help them', said Alec, 'if they produce more.'

Stella climbed back into bed, pressed up against him, considered; and got out again. She ran down to the garden on bare feet and walked on the grass in the autumn dew. A mallard drake with smart military chevrons of a beautiful dark blue was standing on the lawn regarding her.

'Hello,' she said.

The drake moved impatiently from one dark webbed foot

to another, and turned his head about. He had a proprietorial look. At this time in the morning the garden was his. He quacked.

Up on the wall top behind Stella, the stone wall was caked with old ivy. From inside it the kerfuffle began again, and two points of angry light shone out: the eyes of another duck. This duck and the drake glared at Stella, pinpointing her between them, like searchlights.

The wild rebellion within the ivy ceased. The drake flew away and Stella went back to the house.

'Alec! There *are* ducklings,' she said. 'I heard them. I knew it! She's trying to throw them out of the nest down behind the greenhouse and they're complaining.'

Over a silent breakfast she said, 'You know, I thought Lester might have stayed in with us. His last day. I suppose he did come in last night?'

At once, without a word, Alec left the table and went upstairs.

He came down again carrying the double bass. 'He's there,' he said, 'or anyway there's a hump in the bed. This'll have to go in, I suppose. Do you know if he's taking his bike?'

'Ask him.'

'He's dead to the world.'

'If he is taking the bike, he'll have to help you get it up on the car rack,' she said. 'With your back. What about the double bass?'

'Your guess is, as they say, as good as mine. I'll leave it around.'

*

Stella finished packing Lester's suitcases and Alec carried them to the car. After lunch – Lester had just come down and was drinking Coke at the kitchen table – Stella went to the garage carrying Lester's heavy video recorder and computer and boxes of loose tapes. This took three journeys and on the third one, a mother duck marched confidently out from behind the greenhouse, followed by twelve thistledown balls on legs. They rippled behind her in a wavering string.

She hissed at Stella, and her babies squeaked and cheeped like schoolchildren on a nature walk.

Stella lowered the computer to the ground.

Alec's voice shouted from the garage, 'I've got the bike on top, but we'll never get the ruddy double bass in. Where is the damned boy? What's he doing?'

Stella stretched her hand towards the immaculate ducklings who at once rushed to their mother and clustered round her feet like a pulsating soft cushion, and Stella saw that the mother duck was not in fact confident at all. It was bravado. This was her most desperate moment. 'Open the door,' said the duck's black, manic eye. 'The door into the lane.'

She seemed to know where it was and set off towards it.

Stella followed and opened the door. With a serenade of quacking and squeaking the mother duck passed through followed by the long string of her perfect children. In a minute the whole parade had vanished into the greenery along the bank of the stream. A minute more, and there was a gentle splash followed by smaller splashes, as light as raindrops.

Stella noticed the drake then, standing some way along the towpath watching. Then he, too, vanished into the reeds. There was a sense of completion.

'Alec!' She ran to the garage. 'Alec – did you hear them? I *saw* them! There were twelve. They've all swum off down the stream. The drake watched.'

'You weren't dreaming, I suppose?'

'I don't dream about ducklings. Or about anything now.'

He struggled with the double bass, but it resisted a back seat in the car. He swore. Lester was somehow present, looking on and eating a pie.

Alec quite suddenly gave up. 'If you're taking the double bass,' he said, 'there won't be room for all of us.'

'OK,' said Lester.

'So I shall stay at home. Right?'

'Oh, OK. Right,' said Lester. 'Thanks, Dad. Bye, Dad,' and he crawled into the back of the small car. He was a huge young man.

'Oh, Lester.' Stella saw that Alec's hands were shaking. Alec was wearing what he wore only for weddings: a suit and tie. She had put on a dress and jacket. Neither knew much about colleges and they had not been sure whether they would be introduced to the principal. 'Oh, Lester.' In the wing mirror, Stella saw Lester's face looking relieved that his father was not coming.

'If I'd had a few driving lessons,' her son said, 'I needn't have bothered you.'

'Thank you! But we need the car ourselves. Your father

has fastened the bike on top,' she said. 'All alone,' she added.

Alec lifted the double bass into the front seat and Stella clipped herself in behind the wheel.

'Thanks, Dad. See you later, Dad,' said Lester.

'Good luck then,' said Alec at the very last moment, just as the car turned into the lane, and Stella saw him come out after them and stand in the middle of the lane and wave to them; and she thought how thin Alec looked, his wrists skinny inside his suit. He was calling something after them, but they couldn't hear him.

We were old to have a child, she thought.

And she hated Lester. This Lester. She longed for the Lester who used to come in cheerful from school shouting, 'Mum? I'm home, Mum. Can I go out now?' Or, 'You in, Mum? I'm top again.' Or, 'Mum, where's Dad? Is he going fishing?' Or, 'I bought this for you, Mum.'

She longed for the earlier Lester who liked her to read to him in bed. 'Go on, Mum. Don't stop now. Go *on*!' Or the earlier-still Lester, heavy and warm and teething; on her shoulder as she patted his back. Or the newborn Lester who had lain in his pram, gazing in wonder. Wonder at everything. At his own wrists. At leaves across the window, at the eyes of the cat, at the flames in the fire. The Lester who had stroked her face as he fed from her breast.

They had reached the campus of the raw, new university. It was scarcely an hour from home but Stella had never been inside its wrought-iron gates, which were about the only things that appeared to be finished. Lester had only been

there once, last year for the interview. She drove cautiously
through a treeless desolation of pink tarmac, tentatively
round weedy roundabouts. Mud and workmen's tools were
everywhere. Cement kerbstones held back rubble and were
ticketed with signs and arrows for the future. In the distance
there seemed to be a complex of drab prefabricated single-
storey buildings. This was the wider world that Stella had
been so proud that Lester was clever enough to inhabit.

In the back, Lester thought, Oh, Christ, it's dire. Media
Studies. I'm doing Media Studies. I don't have a clue about
Media Studies. I ought to be doing Music. In a proper place.
Why didn't they suggest Music? They never suggest
anything, my parents. They are uninterested. They turned
sort of humble after I got all those A levels. They just *do*
things for me, they never think *of* me. *They are not interested
in Lester*, only in what Lester is *like*. When I was young they
cared about my happiness. Now it's all ironing shirts. And
I'll bet they'll go out for dinner tonight when they've got
rid of me. Well, I'm not staying here, in this place, right?
It's hell.

'Where do you think we go?' she asked him.

He didn't know.

As he sat silent in the back, she again examined her son in
the driving mirror. The shaven head. The nose ring.

He is a huge soft fledgling, she thought. Some sort of
doleful young owl. And he's fat.

And utterly conventional, she thought. Totally self-absorbed. He has no feelings. You can't get near him!

Some students in black tracksuits came running by, their faces screwed up against the fine rain that had started to fall. One of them turned back.

'Oh,' she called, 'could you tell us where to go? I'm bringing my son. It's his first term. Could you tell us where we have to – report?'

'Sure,' said the wet runner and then, 'Oh, hi, Les.'

'Hi,' said Lester and broke from the shell of the car in one grateful spring. He walked round to the front and lifted out the double bass. 'Bye, then, Ma. Thanks for the lift. See you.'

'*What?*' she called after him. '*What?* Lester! Am I not even going to see your *room*?'

''Bye, Ma,' and he loped after his friend.

'What about the bike?' she shouted. 'All the luggage? The computers? Do I take it all home again?'

She started the car, roared after him, catching him and his mate up outside the prefabs. '*Lester!* I will not be treated like this. Take your stuff out of my car and get the bike down. At *once*.'

'OK, Ma. Keep your hair on.'

The two boys piled Lester's possessions inside the tatty building. They seemed a little subdued and she sat on, not moving from her seat in the car.

'*Right*,' she said, switching on the engine. 'You can just get on with it, Lester. I've done my bit and so has your father,' and she drove off.

*

Then, some way down the pitiless asphalt in the gathering
dark, she stopped the car again and rested her head against
the steering wheel. A huge tract of her life passed sadly by.

Feet came padding.

'Ma! Hey, Ma? What's the matter? Don't cry. Ma –? Love
you, Ma.'

'I'm delighted to hear it,' she wept.

'Ma, I'll be coming home at the weekend you know.'

'What?' (Oh, how her heart leapt!) '*Will* you? You didn't
tell us.'

'Of course I am. I'm coming home every weekend for
the next three years. Didn't I say?'

And he saw her heart sink now. Like a stone.

Snap

At three o'clock in the morning over a hundred miles from home in a hotel I'd never heard of before that weekend, I broke my ankle in the bathroom of the en-suite bedroom where I was spending the night with my lover.

He was my first lover. For thirty years I have been married to my husband, Ambrose, who was not my lover before marriage. We were both virgins. I had never been unfaithful to him before that night.

My husband is a highly respected philatelist, often at foreign auctions and stamp collectors' conferences. He is also what is called a music buff and goes to the opera all over Europe. I am not interested in stamps and like to listen to music alone, even though it was at a concert that we met.

He was sitting in front of me and my friend Lizzie Fisher and I thought, What an enormous head! It's like Beethoven's.

It turned out that Lizzie Fisher knew him – she'd had a spell being interested in stamps – and she introduced us and I thought, What an exalted face. He looks like a saint.

Over the long years of our marriage he has been away from me a great deal.

And he was to be away the night of my infidelity, which was my birthday and which he had forgotten. I could see that he was rather troubled about forgetting my birthday and he said he would buy tickets for us to go to Glyndebourne some time to make up for it. He can always get tickets. He still went away.

For the past year or so I have allowed myself to take a tangential view of music and since my friend Lizzie Fisher had started to go to evening classes at the local school of art, and since I'd always secretly believed that I'd be rather good at sculpture, we both enrolled in the modelling class, where it turned out that I was hopeless and Lizzie – as usual – rather good. However, the teacher was kind to me. Often he came up and pushed me aside from what I was trying to do and with one flick of the knife he would turn it into something presentable. Even nice. I would gasp and he would look sideways at me and smile. He spent time with me and the others began to notice. The model in particular noticed. She was a beautiful Croatian girl, brown, hard, flat, silent and twenty. I heard soon that he'd been 'seeing her' for over a year and she was wild for him. I could feel her big fierce eyes on me. But Geoffrey – the teacher – paid no attention and looked at me if anything with more affection.

At the break in each class we'd all go to the canteen where Lizzie Fisher and I would always sit apart from the others, being older than them. After the first term Lizzie Fisher gave up because she was bored. She'd found she was good at modelling the human figure and so began to look for something else. She'd been like this ever since we'd met at college long ago.

But I kept on going and I took my coffee break by myself. The day I discovered that Ambrose had forgotten my birthday and was off to Bayreuth I sat as far away from the others as possible and stirred my coffee and thought that it was years – years and years – since Ambrose had even touched me, let alone looked at my body, or made love to me. He had never been very keen on it, even at the beginning. He got through it as fast as he could, but in an abstracted way as if he was listening for distant music and could only spare a very short time.

Geoffrey came over to my table that evening and sat with me, and I looked up and saw the model drinking her mug of coffee in her silk kimono and bare feet, standing with the students all around her, all of them aware that she was naked under the kimono. Geoffrey sat with his back to them all and looked only at me. And she knew it.

And knew it when he put his long fingers over mine.

Towards the end of the term, just before my birthday, he put his hand over mine again and said, 'Sleep with me.'

'There's a hotel in the Lake District,' he said.

'The Lake District? But it's nearly Scotland!'

'I have to go to Edinburgh. I can drive back through the Lake District. You can drive north from here. For the Friday night. The next morning I'm flying from Manchester to the Paris Exhibition.'

'Of *course* I can't –.'

'Then what chance is there for us?' he said. 'Ever. . . . This is a God-sent chance.'

I didn't think that a hundred-mile journey to the Lake

District to an unknown hotel was a God-sent chance. What if he didn't turn up? I'd have to ask Lizzie Fisher what to do.

But then I thought that this was my own life. It was time I stopped depending on Lizzie Fisher. This was new. It was newer and truer than my marriage thirty years ago, the predictable marriage of *such* a nice girl to *such* a kind and distinguished man. 'Brilliant! Quite brilliant! And so well off. So respected in the Sacred Music world, and in Stamps. She's very lucky.'

I felt odd when Ambrose left for Bayreuth on the Friday morning. He would be away for a week. He was silent and seemed a little dazed. He gave me a peck and patted the dog's head, but he didn't ask what I was doing over my birthday. I suppose he thought I'd go out with Lizzie Fisher. She's the nearest I've got to family. The previous evening I had packed for him while he was in the garden. He meditates every evening for a quarter of an hour, the dog pacing behind him. I watched them coming slowly, slowly up the steps through the water gardens, Ambrose's head bowed, and I thought, He's getting old. How can I?

But I did. As soon as the taxi had driven off I was upstairs and putting things into a suitcase for myself. My car was full of petrol. I turned off the hot water and left lights arranged to come on when it got dark. I checked all the window catches and pressed the answerphone button on the telephone. Only one night.

Then I thought, But suppose he decides to surprise me?

To come back? Or have flowers delivered for my birthday tomorrow?

So I wrote a note, just in case, and propped it on the hall table. *Gone away with Lizzie Fisher.*

I thought of telling Lizzie Fisher everything, but I couldn't. I tried to leave a message on her answerphone but it wasn't switched on so I wrote another, very unnoticeable, note and left it on the front doorstep with a pebble on it, saying, *Please leave any parcels in the greenhouse.*

Then I suddenly saw the dog, lying at the foot of the stairs.

It is unbelievable that I had forgotten the dog, but it is true. He is Ambrose's dog and called Ludwig, and looks ridiculously like Ambrose. I feed, walk, brush and deflea Ludwig, but he loves only Ambrose. He was watching me intently, a huge-headed shining black labrador, now of a certain age.

I'd have to take him with me. Hatred at my heart, I shoved him into the car.

And drove off.

It was the unbearable M6, all round Birmingham. There is an effective route that cuts out Birmingham on the way to the Lake District. I am not sure of it, but I did my best, the lorries bearing down on me like leviathans seeking whom they might devour. I did not care, though Ludwig seemed restless. It was Friday afternoon and the weekend world was racing towards its breakneck break.

I reached the Lake District safely and drove between the purple mountains and the crowds taking photographs beside the silver waters. The hotel stood on its own upon a green hillside. What *was* I doing? The dog lay asleep in the back with its four black legs in the air.

And of course Geoffrey wasn't there.

I waited a while, in the car park. Then I fed Ludwig off a tin plate I'd brought with a tin of Chum, and took him for a walk up behind the hotel and gazed down at the ridiculously beautiful backdrop of Causey Pike. What could I do tomorrow to fill the time? There was the Wordsworth Museum at Grasmere. Or Beatrix Potter.

The evening grew cold and grey, and the lake waters slapped bad-temperedly about, so I heaved myself up – my bones are no longer the bones of a girl – and back in the car park Ludwig growled and his hair rose behind the ears and I saw a small, furtive-looking man in awful cheap clothes scurrying about near the entrance.

So I went round the side of the hotel, shutting Ludwig in the car. I went in and sat in the lounge and read a newspaper.

People were all around, happily chattering. There was a group of two amiable families, noisy and pleased with each other, discussing old times over tea and cakes. After a while in came the unrecognisable Geoffrey and for a second he seemed uncertain. He too looked surprised as I lowered the newspaper. 'Oh! Hi!' he said. I hadn't realised he was so short. And so common.

But the dinner was good, and the wine, and he lost his abstracted expression and in the lounge drinking brandies – the two families now decidedly rowdy and all still knocking back the tea – he put his hand over mine once more and said, 'Shall we go up?'

I said, 'I must see to the dog.'

He said, 'The *dog*?'

'Must take him for his walk around.'

'*Dog?*'

'Yes. He's in the car. Ludwig.'

'Oh. I see.'

'I'll not take long,' and I ran to the car and let Ludwig sniff around and patted him, but when I tried to put him back he began to howl and he wouldn't stop. He leapt about the car over the seats howling for Ambrose like some singer at Bayreuth. I had to take him into the hotel and he dominated the entrance hall.

'He won't settle in the car.'

'Well, they won't let him in the bedrooms,' said Geoffrey.

'Oh, of course we will,' said the concierge. 'Would he like a blanket?'

'He usually sleeps on a bit of blanket,' I said. 'At home.'

Geoffrey was examining the watercolours on the walls.

'Well, we do *have* a bit of blanket,' said the concierge and we trooped up to bed.

Ludwig took a long time settling his blanket to his satisfaction. Then he scuffled about and snorted and farted and yawned. Finally he slept or seemed to sleep, but he whimpered in his dreams.

At last he was quiet, and Geoffrey got down to what we had come for and I thought, Oh yes! *Yes!* I remember! Oh, I love this! Oh Geoffrey! and Geoffrey made similar loud observations, and Ludwig awoke in consternation and leapt on the bed. He is a large and heavy dog, and Geoffrey I'd not realised is very slight. There was a tussle.

'Put the bloody thing in the bathroom,' said Geoffrey and I did, turning off the bathroom light and saying soothing things to Ludwig. I didn't feel anything against him. I almost felt love. I hadn't considered he might ever feel protective towards me.

Geoffrey fell asleep at once and, much later, I fell asleep too and then of course I woke. I am no longer twenty years old and I do sometimes have to get up in the night. I crept out of bed, opened the bathroom door, felt for the string to turn the light on, fell over the dog, and my feet flew from under me and one of them *hit* the further wall, only inches away, wham!

I heard the snap. My foot was gone. It hung down like a leaf. Ludwig, his protective instincts exhausted, padded from the bathroom and back to his blanket.

I knew it was broken.

At first I felt no pain at all but when I leaned forward to touch it there were vibrations everywhere like silent aeolian strings. They trembled up and down, back and front, over the toes, up each side of the leg and up the back of the shin. It wasn't a 'twisted ankle'. It wasn't what in the Girl Guides we had called a 'sprain' and had learned to treat. This ankle was broken. Smash, snap!

I crawled into the bedroom and heaved myself on to the bed, and Geoffrey lay there deeply sleeping. But something woke him and he turned his head and opened his eyes and he looked at me, mystified. He'd had a lot of wine.

I said, 'Geoffrey. I think I've broken my ankle,' and he said 'Oh, no!' and sank to sleep again.

Beside the bedside telephone there was a number to ring the front desk; but nobody answered. I tried again and got a metallic voice telling me that there was nobody there until 6.30 a.m. but in an emergency to ring ... And he babbled out a number so fast that I couldn't hear it though I tried three times. I think then that I passed out.

I woke to Geoffrey's packing (Ludwig was deep asleep) and it was seven o'clock and he was off to Manchester airport. He kissed my cheek. I said, 'So sorry, Geoffrey. I'm afraid I broke my ankle,' and he said, 'Oh, no!'

I said,' Don't go to Paris.'

He said, 'Paris? I'm not going to Paris. I'm going to Zagreb.'

'You're so beautiful,' he said, 'and so innocent. I'll tell them at the desk,' and he was gone.

In time I got help. They were excellent and so apologetic about the emergency number.

They were sending for an ambulance and I would be well looked after. The Lake District was the perfect place to break an ankle. The mountain rescue were on twenty-four-hour call. The nearest hospital was thirty-five miles away at Carlisle, but it was first class. They would telephone anyone I wanted. Had I children?'

No, I had no children. And there was the dog.

'Ah – the dog.'

'Your – partner – settled the bill last night. He thought this morning that you might have a friend –?'

I knew that I did not want Lizzie Fisher to know. And what purpose to ring Ambrose in Bayreuth? I took a deep breath and said, 'D'you know, my car's an automatic. This is my left foot. I believe I can drive myself home.'

'It is out of the question,' they said, but I saw what a relief it would be for them if I simply disappeared.

'Could you get me a wheelchair to the car and someone to help me wash and dress – and put the dog in?'

'We could, but we'd be most –.'

'Oh, please.'

Someone came and helped me into the bathroom, where I closed my eyes.

And they lifted me into the car, put Ludwig in behind me, where he rested his smelly black jaw on my shoulder. They brought me a thermos of coffee. From the pretty Swiss gables of the hotel faces peered, the two indefatigable families venturing a distant interest. The mountains brooded on.

Now, the driver of a car is usually two people (or a single schizophrenic). One of them is terrified, watchful of every other vehicle as a potential enemy; every other driver is about to swerve, overtake, fall asleep, attack and destroy. The other self is confident, skilled and in charge, and this second covert creature comes to the fore in time of trial. My useless left foot flapped against the hump that occurs down the middle of cars but my right foot behaved like Schumacher's on his best of days. I roared from the Lake District scene, sending Ludwig backwards into a heap behind me. In twenty minutes I was on the motorway, then on the road home. 'How far have you to go?' the hotel had asked. 'No distance at all,' said the Schumacher self. ('And if I die, I die,' said the fallen, defeated mess of a wife.)

Petrol?

I stopped. I could not get out, so I hooted and eventually a fat girl came waddling.

'I've hurt my foot. I can't get out. Can you get me some petrol? I'll have to pay with a card.'

'If you pay by card you have to come inside to activate your pin.'

'Can you find me the manager? I can't activate my pin.'

'There isn't a manager.'

'Then I shall call the police.'

She said, 'Just a minute,' and disappeared for ten, returning with someone holding an electronic pin machine.

I roared on, took a wrong turning and found myself on the Birmingham ring road, which again I flew along to a chorus of wailing horns and cartoon-strip purple, yelling faces. I left at the correct exit and thundered on, cameras flashing, motorists blaring, the road vanishing beneath me and far away behind.

I did not stop.

I was desperate to pee, but it went off.

I hung on.

And I reached home.

The house was as dead as when I had left it the previous day. The note under the pebble guarding against possible flowers had not been disturbed. I turned off the engine and began to cry.

Then the pain began, grabbing me like a manacle. It was the devil's grip and he was saying to me, 'Ha-ha! I am here! You have sinned. You have sinned against your good, kind husband to please a rat. You are also a fool. You should have gone to hospital. You may be in plaster now for months. A wheelchair case. You may limp for the rest of your life. You are now, officially, an old woman. You have "had a fall".'

So in my weedless semicircular drive this summer morning I leaned back in my seat and wept. It was not yet eleven o'clock. I'd driven from the Lake District in two hours. Now I could not get out of the car, for a huge conflagration was raging inside my shoeless flapping foot.

I wept on and the postman came up the drive and gave me a jaunty wave. He stopped only when Ludwig set up a howl to waken the dead. Ludwig howled and barked and battered his paws against all the windows, and the postman paused and looked in.

He is a big man and I am small. He lifted me out and, still holding me, found the house keys in my bag and opened the door. He laid me gently on the sofa in the hall and got on to his mobile for an ambulance.

'But I am safe now,' I said. (And nobody need ever know.) I leaned over to the hall table to pull away the note I'd left saying I'd gone off with Lizzie Fisher and tore it up.

Sounds outside indicated the ambulance and the postman came back saying he'd left the dog next door – yes, quite agreeable. 'We'll soon have you right,' he said and dropped a letter on my chest.

Thick expensive writing paper. Posted yesterday, the envelope handwritten in Ambrose's tense, consistent fountain-pen script. I knew at once it must have been written before he left and posted from the airport. The stamp was stuck on very straight.

The ambulance crew were examining my ankle, gently touching while they watched my face. Someone was giving me an injection of morphine in the arm. 'It doesn't stop the pain, love, but it stops you caring about it.'

I said, 'Thank you,' and opened the letter which began, *All I can do is tell you the truth without preamble. It has been over for so long, has it not? In the end I have made the decision to go away with Lizzie Fisher.*

The Last Reunion

B renda was keeping on about how she and Stafford had met for the first time at this very place, at this same time of year, and how she had never slept with any other man and how they'd both been virgins at their wedding and how now, over forty years on, they were proud of it.

Eileen, a smouldering woman, was thinking about where Lily would park the car. There had been no instructions.

Lily, who was driving the car, her cherry-coloured Alfa Romeo, was wondering why she was filled with heaviness: a heaviness unnatural to her, though natural enough for Eileen. It was Eileen's almost permanent condition and ever had been. Eileen had been silent at college and silent she remained. Eileen looked like a storm. In fact, Eileen's black brows and suspicious mouth and barrel figure reflected an even greater darkness at sixty-plus than in the student. Though for no obvious reason. Eileen's life since graduation had been highly respected, diligent and secure. She had been a secretary somewhere at the Foreign Office, never late with a memo; and she was considered rather a splendid institution once you'd become used to the expression of suppressed fury on her face.

The fourth woman, Elizabeth, was edging dreamily towards Alzheimer's.

Beautiful at nineteen, Elizabeth had left college at the end of her first year to marry someone from Devonshire with horses. All the year she had been in love with a Polish Jew called Ernie, a physicist she'd met at the inter-collegiate Freshers' hop the first night. And all that year on the college tennis courts the beautiful equality and power of the base-line returns of Elizabeth and Ernie had haunted the evening hours, as other girls sat at desks in their rooms above, trying to keep their windows shut against the laughter.

The year Elizabeth had been with Ernie her looks had lit dark places. She had shone in the rhododendron alley, in the grotto by the lake, in the backstreet café they all used to visit on Wednesdays after lectures on *Paradise Lost*. She had shone along the dark road back to the college at night after the theatre, several girls together eating chips out of paper — though Elizabeth didn't eat chips.

'Look at that *girl*!' you heard said sometimes as Elizabeth passed under a street light. 'Did you *see* that girl?' At a time when women English Literature students were all trying to look like Virginia Woolf, Elizabeth effortlessly did so, but with an unselfconscious happiness Virginia Woolf never managed.

It had been a great surprise to meet Elizabeth again today, for even Brenda had twenty years earlier stopped sending Christmas cards marked 'Kindly forward if necessary'. None of them had seen her since the Finals ball at the end of their third year, though Elizabeth, who had left after three terms (with a First in Part One and acrimony from the college), had had no right whatever to be at the Finals ball. She had brought her husband Rupert with her. A genial soul. They had left early.

The other three had danced all night. Then they had

walked with their partners – one being Brenda's Stafford –
to the green side-gate that led into the public park. They
had walked – Lily entwined – as far as the bridge over the
canal, said their goodbyes, walked back again and been
checked in by a woman called the Home Tutor, Miss Folly.
She had had a notebook and a cape and purple stockings,
her habitual garb even at sunrise. Alert Miss Folly had seen
them in by the gate like a milkmaid letting through the little
heifers soon to be off to the slaughter of the world.

That sleepy, rose-blown morning forty years ago the three
girls had drifted back via the grounds, up the stone steps
between the Italian urns, across the lawns, in through the
glass doors. Long dresses had been soaked with dew. Lily,
who had spent most of the night inside the skirts of a large
willow, entangled in strong arms, had been barefoot and
tipsy, balancing about on her toes. Poor Brenda had been in
a daze of love for Stafford. Eileen had been thoughtful and
terse. Her partner had been somebody's faceless brother who
hadn't made much of her.

So that was that. Tomorrow they would be scattered. Six
weeks later would come their Finals results. Six weeks after
that, up would come to the college the next intake of fledgling schoolgirls, hesitant or bold, plain or pretty, stupid or
clever, and one or maybe two 'remarkable'. Of these four
now elderly women only Elizabeth had been in any way
remarkable.

And Elizabeth, who could have done anything, had kept her
secrets. Why she had left. Where Ernie, the Polish physicist,

had gone and why. Nobody knew or felt they could ask; young women then were shy with each other.

The four girls had all read English Literature. Brenda had then taught it, Eileen had ditched it, Lily had tried to write it, and Elizabeth had drifted off to Barnstaple, not with Ernie but with Rupert, and had had five children and not much else.

And now Elizabeth sat in the front of Lily's Alfa Romeo saying 'What a lovely car,' while Eileen sat glum in the back with Brenda chatting of chastity.

Lily was turning now through the main gates of the college, the same black-and-gold scroll about them saying *Semper Eadem*. Now the car was winding down the college drive between much taller trees than they remembered, and Eileen was sighing and grunting and asking why they had come. She hated reunions.

The college was a women's college, one hundred years old, and it was closing down. Or rather it was amalgamating with a male college and moving to Leicestershire. The wonderful buildings, the great lawns, the avenues of trees, the botanic garden, the science laboratories had been bought by American bankers to train financial moguls from the Pacific Rim in the philosophy of money. Invitations to a final reunion had been sent out long ago by a committee, to such old students as had kept in touch, and there had been wide advertisement about it in the press. So hundreds, maybe thousands, of women were expected.

Coachloads of them from way before the war were arriving

from all parts of the country, said Lily, who wrote fiction.

'God help us all,' said Eileen.

The day chosen for the reunion had been the day after Finals. The day after the final Finals of the college. The anniversary of the day of the rose-petal skirts in the dew, the strawberries and cream supper and the gentle Bucks Fizz, of the band that had played selections from *South Pacific*, of the goodbyes upon the little bridge and Miss Folly in purple. The day of the last breakfast together through the glass doors, of baked apples on oak tables, of servants in cap and apron who had served the baked apples at 6 a.m. And there had been silver toast racks.

Still in their long dresses that long-ago morning, some girls had gone trailing away to bed and others had gone outside again holding each other's hands (you could then) and talking of men (you did then) and of what was going to happen next.

Brenda had lifted her certain face to the sun and said, 'He's asked me,' and Lily, half asleep, had said, 'Are you going to?'

'Oh yes. We'll do it at once I should think. Before next term. We'll both be at the same teacher-training, after all.'

'Do it?' said Eileen. 'Do what?'

'Well, marry,' said Brenda, firm and triumphant. Intolerable.

'Think of him in bed,' Lily whispered sideways (nasty) to Dilys Something, an awful girl wild for power, rich and humourless. She'd been at the ball with someone famous

everybody thought they ought to recognise although he'd
looked like almost everybody else. Nobody had ever heard
of either of them again.

'He'll have one like a pencil,' said Lily, and Dilys stared.

'Where's Elizabeth gone?' black-browed Eileen asked.

'Oh, home,' said Lily, 'ages ago. Where've you been? She
said goodbye to us all. You're slipping.'

For Eileen had been a logbook.

And now, today, the last reunion, and here were the direc-
tions to the car park, about turn: off down the drive again
to the end, out into a huge, roped-off area outside the
grounds. It would be a quarter-mile walk back. Eileen looked
satisfied. She'd known there'd be trouble parking but
nobody ever listened to her. Of course.

Lily said, 'Can you walk it, Eileen?'

'No need to be unpleasant.'

'Well, I know you've got a knee. We could have dropped
you off.'

'I told you,' said Eileen, thumping away. 'I'm OK. You'd
better lock the car.'

Lily, who had been about to, said there was no need. Not
to fuss. It was all by invite. Old girls. Nobody here would
be nicking cars.

'Want to bet?' said Eileen's square old back.

There were vehicles of every kind, and every kind and age
of woman. Some were staring about them, some were
greeting and exclaiming, some were putting their heads back

inside their cars again to bring out picnics and sticks and Zimmers. Some were roaring up on mopeds, unfastening great medieval helmets and looking about sixteen. Some were pacing arm in arm, careful of the paths. Some were undoing pushchairs, humping children about. Lily set off after limping Eileen, and Brenda followed behind until she remembered hesitant Elizabeth and went back for her. The Virginia Woolf dazzle was long gone from Elizabeth now, but there was still a bewildered sweetness.

A surge of talk and laughter met them as they came to the steps behind the urns. Over the lawns above, hundreds of women were scattered like beads. 'The noise!' shrieked Brenda joyfully. 'The noise!'

And Lily thought, I shouldn't have come. I cannot bear it. I hate this sort of thing. But I will not let Eileen win. Though God knows, she's right.

Women sprawled in groups on rugs. Some had brought wine. Others like schoolgirls were in jeans, eating out of plastic bags, with rings in their noses. Others had pearls in their ears. Some wore lipstick and floating skirts, and had had their hair done. Some looked determinedly dirty and ill and scornful and hip. Some carried handbags. Some peered down into cameras. Some carried photograph albums of grandchildren. There paced the present principal, unknown to Lily and co., ready for Leicester, eagle of eye, in a silk suit. There went a white-haired woman in a long tea gown and Doc Martens and a hat.

'There are some really old ones over there; best keep away,' said Lily. 'I remember those basket chairs. They've brought them out of the bursar's room. It was all basket chairs and hyacinths. She wore paisley shawls. There was an ivory cigarette box. She'll be dead now.'

'She was dead then,' said Eileen, 'and they can't be the same chairs.'

'There's no organisation,' said Brenda. 'They haven't even tried. Talk about the last day in the old home. You can hear the removal vans revving up round the corner. There's not even tea. What's that banner doing? There are all sorts of *banners*, it's like a rally.'

'That one says *Social Studies*,' said Lily. 'Whatever are "Social Studies"?'

'What the thick ones did,' said Eileen, 'the spotty ones with the dirty hair. You could always tell the sociologists.'

'Thanks a bunch,' said a skeleton with glinting ringlets of Afro gold lying about at Lily's feet on the grass. 'That's what I am.'

She looked about ten. Beside her was hunched a bored and venerable man with massive shoulders, who hung his head and clasped his hands about his knees.

Brenda inspected him with surprise. 'I didn't know we could bring husbands. Well, I do think that should have been made clear. I met my husband, Stafford, here, you know. More than forty years ago and at *exactly* this time of year.' She sat down on the grass. 'You go on,' she said to the other three. 'I'll stay with these younger ones for a moment.'

Brenda was a year younger than the others, having been precocious at school. 'They're older than me,' she told the sociologist and the thinker. 'I came up early. I should really have stayed and tried for Oxford but I was impatient. Thank *goodness* or I would never have met Stafford. When did you come down? You look almost young enough not to have come up yet.'

'In 1970,' said the girl. 'I've been with my husband twenty years in the Third World.'

'Well, my goodness! I must say it suits you. I do apologise. I'm hopeless at ages, I suppose because I simply can't believe in my own. Between ourselves, I feel about twenty-seven.'

But the ancient husband had climbed to his feet and given his hand to the girl. They walked away.

'Well, their manners are not ours even if they have been married twenty years and she doesn't call him partner,' said Brenda. 'Sociologists were always short on manners. I suppose they have to be like the clients.'

In the circle of basket chairs about a dozen cobwebby people were sitting under the English Literature banner. One appeared to be asleep. You could see it was an exclusive circle set apart from the mêlée, for conversation was nominal and the champagne was Grand Cru. It was the English Faculty.

Eileen, Brenda and Lily stood, feeling younger but sad. 'D'you recognise anyone? There can't be any of ours left.'

'I think the sleeping one's drunk,' said Eileen.

Suddenly Elizabeth spoke. 'It's Dr Blatt,' she said and went across all smiles, and knelt on the grass. 'Dr Blatt? It's Elizabeth.'

'Hello,' said Dr Blatt, opening an eye. 'Oh, hello, Elizabeth. I never see anyone these days. I'm always in Bodley.'

Others in the circle of dons looked up at the quartet of their long-ago students, but without significant interest. Lily and glowering Eileen hovered. Brenda would have liked to speak, but found herself a bit uncertain of how to bring in Stafford.

'I think that one's Folly,' Lily said to Brenda, and Miss Folly looked up brightly and raised her glass. She had not changed until you looked again and saw the map of the years, the purple hands and fat ankles. Her black braids were scanty and grey but she was still wearing coloured stockings.

'This must be a sad day for you,' said Lily.

'No, no. Not at all. We must move on. We were always leasehold, you know. It is time to be out of the ivory tower. I, of course, retired years ago. To become a nun.'

'You made it a very beautiful ivory tower,' said Lily, remembering red leaves and dahlias in a gold jug, and a blue velvet chair, and six or seven Lear etchings pinned haphazardly down the side of a rosewood bookcase in the tutor's old rooms. 'I remember your Lears,' she said, and got a strange look.

'There was a suicide on her floor,' whispered Eileen. 'While she was entertaining a drip of a priest on a mandolin.'

Elizabeth asked Dr Blatt if she would come to tea with her yesterday and old Professor Alice Grimwade – once her junior tutor – watched them go off together, Elizabeth pushing the chair. 'That girl with Alzheimer's,' she said. 'I remember her. She knew her Tragedies. There are so few intellectuals coming up now. They all want to go into the City.'

'She's side-stepped tragedies,' said Eileen.

'That is the remark of a fool, Miss Belling.'

And Eileen blushed. Miss Grimwade had even remembered her name.

'You have kept in touch with Elizabeth Vaughan then, have you Miss Belling? Miss Dodds?'

'We haven't seen her from her last day to this last day,' said Brenda. 'It was Lily who heard from her. Elizabeth wrote to Lily's publisher. Elizabeth asked us to meet her off the train. When we saw her – well, we saw –'

'Tragedy, I fear. Well, it was our tragedy that she left. Why didn't you stop her, Lily Strang? You were always timid. But you've kept your maiden name for your books, I see.'

'I'm not exactly Mrs Gaskell.'

'No,' said Professor Grimwade.

Two younger women standing waiting for audience nearby, one holding a baby, the other struggling with a two-year old, looked jolted and tried to remember Mrs Gaskell. At the same moment they realised that Lily Strang must be 'Lily Strang', whose novels sold all over the world in twenty-seven languages and were in every supermarket beside the sweets. When you looked, you could see the earrings could be Hermès. They turned hastily to the professor.

'I just wanted to say, Professor Grimwade, after all this time – to thank you for your lectures on Eliot.'

'We were here in 1984,' said the other, grabbing her child who had begun to crawl about among the academic legs. 'It was after one of your lectures that I had almost a mystical experience – I really *discovered* Eliot. Under that tree.'

'I wonder what he was doing?' said the professor and held Lily's gaze as if daring her to say: Maybe he was spread out like *a patient etherised upon a –*

Lily didn't.

'You really, honestly, so inspired us,' said the first woman hitching up her baby against her chest in his harness.

'Dear child,' said the professor, and became thoughtful. 'Have you read Miss Strang's novels? They are very entertaining.'

'Which', she said after the two mothers had gone, 'is more than *they* are. I often wonder how we managed to choose such dull girls. And such ugly ones. We once chose a girl because she was pretty. No brains, but she did just as well as anyone else.'

Lily felt certain it was her and felt wretched.

'It wasn't you, Miss Strang.'

Then she felt worse.

'Do you remember many of us, Dr Grimwade?'

'No. None. Not at first. Then you say your names and sometimes I see the face through the face. Some of you of course change hardly at all, like poor Eileen Belling. Formed in the cradle.'

'Have I changed?'

'Still changing, Lilian. You were very unformed. I have waited a long time for your fame.'

'I thought I was academic. You might have told me I wasn't. I gather it was pretty obvious.'

'It would have been cruel. You had to find out for yourself,' said the stark old crow.

Brenda had discovered some tea inside the college, through the glass doors, and came back to tell the others. She found Lily, head down and walking very quickly away from the circle of elders.

Eileen was over by the lupin border, sitting staring up at the rows of residential windows. 'I was third along the front,' she said. 'You were seventh along, Brenda.'

'I was sixth,' said Lily.

'No, fifth,' said Eileen, who forgot nothing.

'You forget nothing,' said Lily. 'It must be hard having total recall when all it does is make you so miserable. You ought to see someone about it. Have you thought of it?'

'No,' said Eileen.

She shambled off with Lily towards tea. Elizabeth and Dr Blatt in her wheelchair were nowhere to be seen. Brenda had gone on ahead and was seated at one of the long oak tables of the baked-apple breakfast. They were covered in white heat marks, now, and unpolished. Brenda was talking to a fiftyish-looking woman with a baby on her knees.

'This is Ms Beech,' said Brenda, 'a single parent. How much braver she is than us, though I don't think I could ever have gone along with the idea myself, morally – I'd better be honest. I've been telling her that the last time we sat at these tables was after our Finals ball when my husband

Stafford proposed to me. We have been happily married for over forty years.'

The baby, who had a runny eye but glorious red hair, suddenly reached across Brenda to Eileen's finger and, without taking his eyes off her glowering face, stuck it in his mouth and began to chew it.

'Hey!' said brooding Eileen, and the baby opened his mouth round the finger to laugh. Eileen made a sound like a laugh, too.

'Unfortunately, Stafford and I never had children,' said Brenda, 'though we both adore them and have many godchildren. We were both virgins when we married, you know. It was not unusual then. I'm not sorry about it. And we've never, either of us, ever slept with anyone else, which I expect you must find droll.'

'Well, I've got a baby, thank God,' said Ms Beech.

'I'm not so sure about God,' said Brenda. 'Stafford and I have always been humanists.'

'I'm a woman priest,' said Ms Beech. 'My dead husband was the Bishop of Axminster.'

Lily looked around at the room, the tables, the panelling, all scuffed and sticky. Tea was being dispensed from a machine on the wall into paper cups with optional lids. The paper cups were adding more to the pattern of white rings on the table tops. A few last notices curled from sticky tape on the panelling. The parquet floor was dirty.

'They've been admitting men the last few years,' said Eileen, 'and it shows.'

'I was all against it,' said Brenda. 'I wrote to the governing body. In our time no men were allowed in the building after ten o'clock at night,' she told Ms Beech, 'and they had to be out of our rooms by a quarter to. We worked all the better for it, I'm sure.'

'Why were they more dangerous after nine forty-five?' asked the widowed Reverend Beech.

'We often had to *smuggle* them out,' said Brenda, and the Rev. Beech called upon her God.

'It's true,' said Lily Strang.

'In our year there were some who'd been in the war,' said Brenda. 'They'd been in prison camps and fighting in Africa, and they still had to have their boyfriends out by ten o'clock.'

'There was one who was married,' said Lily, 'and Folly only let her husband in on her birthday.'

'You made that up,' said Brenda.

'She could never tell the truth,' said Eileen. 'Novels were a godsend to her. Kept her out of the courts.'

'Are you Lily Strang?' asked Ms Beech, but said no more when Lily answered yes.

'Stafford loved coming to visit me here,' said Brenda. 'I used to like going with him to the gate. He was so graceful. He'd been in the Army Education Corps. Once it was almost eleven o'clock and anyone could have seen us going to the gate – it was summertime – Folly or anyone. "Don't *scuttle*," he said. "Don't be ashamed." I was in the sixth room along the front.'

'Seventh,' said Eileen.

Ms Beech closed her eyes and the baby was sick.

*

After tea they walked about until Brenda said that she must think about leaving. Stafford would be waiting to hear all about it. And she was really annoyed. She was fed up. She had had no idea that he could have come with her. 'And he's got diabetes now,' she said.

'We can't go yet,' said Lily, 'I have to get Elizabeth back to the station. Really someone ought to see her all the way home – don't you think?'

Nobody answered.

Sour old Eileen said, 'I ought to be getting home myself.'

'Why?'

'Well, I rather want to.'

'You always do. You always want things to be over.'

'I like to think about them afterwards.'

'My God! Are you *old*!'

'I'm depressed,' said Eileen. 'It's my temperament. I can't help it. I knew it would be dreadful and it is. I like being at home. You know me.'

'I do. It is insulting. Why can't we go out to dinner somewhere?'

'There's a programme I want to watch. And I have to read a holiday brochure.'

'When are you going away?'

'Next spring.'

'Far away?'

'Yes. The Isle of Man.'

'Oh, to hell, go home then,' said Lily. 'Go with Brenda. If you're lucky you might get a peep at graceful Stafford waiting at the bus stop. With the dog. Guess the dog? I guess a pug. With filthy breath. Well, I'm glad you can still laugh now and then.'

'You're still infantile, Lily.'

They smiled at each other. They had always been friends.

'Room three,' said Eileen. 'That was my room. I was deflowered in that room the night of the ball.'

'What? *Eileen!* You? No! When?'

'During the supper interval. It was quite a long supper interval. I was famished by morning and only baked apples.'

'However did you get him there? There were ropes on the stairs – I've just remembered that. Didn't anyone see you? Folly in her stockings? *Eileen!*'

'He was quite cunning. Quite . . . inventive.'

'Who was he?'

'I'll tell you one day.'

'It wasn't –? Eileen – no! Oh, Eileen! Oh, poor old Brenda! It was Stafford.'

'Bye, Lily. Don't put it in a book.'

When Eileen had found Brenda, they went off together towards the bus, through the green gate, and Lily went searching for Elizabeth. The starling chatter on the lawns was still loud but spaces were beginning to appear. The flocks were flying. The banners looked lonelier. The Eng. Lit. circle of basket chairs was empty. Dr Blatt could be seen being wheeled off briskly by Miss Folly. Professor Grimwade was gone.

Lily wandered round the science blocks and past the library. One year Queen Mary had paid the college a visit and as she left had stood outside the library beside her great black car, saying goodbye, in the wind. The wind had not disturbed a hair of her head or the toque that was sculpted on to it. Ropes of fat pearls on a ski-slope of bosom, feathers, diamonds. Historic as the czar. Two long lines of students had stood clapping and the sound of the clapping had been like washing blowing on a blustery day. Black washing. Their gowns had fluttered about. Smuts flying from a chimney. 'How *nice* they all look in their little gowns.'

Sycophantic faces framed by half a mile of books had looked down from the tall library windows. What would the bankers do with the library? Make it into a canteen.

Lily walked towards the lake, beside the botanic gardens, into the grotto with the dry fountain. She found a winding path she had forgotten and coming along it towards her was a trim woman of about her own age, who went by, looking down and sideways, with a reserved smile. After she'd gone, Lily realised it was someone called Ellie Simmonds who'd read French and had always had a reserved smile.

Suddenly she was overcome with affection for Ellie Simmonds who had lived with her parents at Potters Bar in a house all mock-Tudor beams and arty latches. She'd invited Lily to stay there for a weekend several years after they'd left college.

Why ever?

They'd played ping-pong with her brothers and made noisy jokes. And into the pillow Lily had sobbed at night, broken-hearted about the one inside the willow, who had left her, and about this terrible step backwards: ping-pong with schoolboys. How on earth had she come to be staying with Ellie Simmonds? Could Ellie Simmonds possibly have guessed?

Think. Think of the one under the willow. Think, Lilian – can you even remember his name? And all that agony. Didn't happen now, presumably. It was the girl who made the running these days. Oh, we were so bottled up and costive and feeble. Oh, we were so *good*!

God – and I wore pink taffeta and sweated under my arms.

She watched the departing back of kind, shy Ellie Simmonds who would still be embarrassed to discuss a broken spirit.

And – God! – long, grey gloves, thought Lily. And a silk rose. A grey silk rose! At twenty-one I was wearing a grey silk rose. It was a nice dress, though. A *Vogue* pattern. He had the most wonderful, gentle hands.

Over towards the tennis courts she found Elizabeth, who was standing beside the posts that had already been dragged out of the ground like teeth and tossed on top of the heaps of black tennis nets piled up like fishing gear on a quay. The tennis courts were to be rebuilt in the new sports complex that was to cover all the lawns.

'We lost you, Elizabeth. Eileen and Brenda had to go.'

Elizabeth came over to her and stood smiling.

'Elizabeth – will you be all right? I'll come all the way home with you on the train if you like. I mean it. I'd like to go to Devon.'

Elizabeth said, 'Train?'

'Train home. I'm Lily. Dear Elizabeth.'

'I know you're Lily. I was thinking. Yes. No – it's all right. Rupert got me a return ticket. He'll meet me. I'm fine. It's very early days, you know. At present. Quite happy. I'm busy packing. Do you remember Ernie? He was a physicist. A Pole.'

'Yes, of course I do.'

Lily took Elizabeth's arm and they started off towards the car park. 'Elizabeth – you don't know how jealous we all were. You were so fearless. So positive. And getting the hell out . . . out of all this college stuff. Getting your life right. Knowing exactly what to do. Even at nineteen. And not coming back –'

'I wasn't fearless,' she said. 'I was a romantic fool. You should all have stopped me.'

'*We* should?'

'Well, *you* could have, Lily. You could have *made* me come back.'

'But you were unapproachable. Olympian. We were scared stiff of you. You were so sure. So wonderful and beautiful.'

'I was a mess.'

Lily said, looking up at the scroll of Latin over the gates, 'You know, it's the *place* I remember. The atmosphere. The Eng. Lit.'s all pretty hazy. All those lectures. All that reading. When I try to remember Keats now, it turns into Shakespeare and Shakespeare's all quotations. All that Anglo-Saxon, I've forgotten the lot.'

'Glad it's not just me,' said Elizabeth. At the car park she said, 'What a wonderful car. Is it yours?'

*

At Paddington station Lily went with her on to the platform to find the reserved first-class seat and several men, some quite young, looked at Elizabeth with admiration and she smiled at them. Then she walked back with Lily, to see her off the platform.

'Bye, Elizabeth,' said Lily. 'It's lovely you came. We'd none of us forgotten you, you know. We never will.'

'Don't count on it,' said Elizabeth, then her face looked blank. Over Lily's head she said, 'I don't suppose you ever see him?'

'Never. For goodness sake, Elizabeth – he was all yours. Utterly yours.'

'Who? *Who* was?'

'Well, *Ernie* of course.'

'Yes, Ernie,' she said. 'Ernie. You see – I had some notion that Ernie might turn up today.'

Acknowledgements

The Virgins of Bruges and *The Latter Days of Mr Jones* were first published in the *Spectator* in 1996 and 2003 respectively. *The Milly Ming*, *Babette* and *Learning to Fly* were Woman's Hour readings on BBC Radio 4, while *Learning to Fly* was published in the *Sunday Express Magazine* in 2000. *Waiting for a Stranger* was published in *Country Life* in 2002.